ONE
CASUAL
CONVERSATION

EDWIN P. MACNICOLL JR.

ISBN: 1533657920
ISBN 13: 9781533657923
Library of Congress Control Number: 2016909403
CreateSpace Independent Publishing Platform
North Charleston, South Carolina

This book is a work of fiction. Any names, characters, places, brands,
media, and incidents are either the product of the author's imagination
or used fictitiously. And any resemblance to actual persons, living or
dead, business establishments, events or locales is entirely coincidental.

This book is dedicated my Grandchildren

It was on a Friday. When I awoke and was having my first cup of coffee as I looked out the window, I started thinking, it was one gorgeous fall day, blue sky and white puffy clouds. It had been raining for a few days and it was great to awaken to this. As I sat there, I felt like I had to do something this weekend.

I was so tired of sitting at home waiting for folks to visit that don't visit. I was not looking forward to another weekend of sitting in the house watching boring TV; no, no more of that, so I thought that I would take a ride up to the Pocono's and spend the weekend by myself, just enjoying the changing of the leaves. So, I got dressed, called for a reservation at our favorite resort, packed some clothes and started to drive.

As I drove, I felt so great, and for a second, I closed my eyes and remembered once again that my late wife Rose and I loved to take this drive every year: usually between November 1st and the 20th.

It seems that after Rose passed, more and more I am all alone. It's not that my children and friends do not love and care for me. Right after the funeral, my children and friends were very concerned and were there for me every day. But as weeks and months passed, they faded. I understand that, after all, they all did have their own lives to live. I noticed that if and when my children stopped by, they fiddled around a bit, talked a little, brought me up to date with their families and then, within a short time, they were gone. If I was invited to a family function, a party or picnic or a family function, it seems I was welcomed and then sat someplace and was forgotten. At least this was the feeling I had.

Oh sure, of course, I knew they loved me, but I felt that my constant talking about their mom (making everyone remember, or referring to her constantly) that without wanting to, I might have upset the kids because it made them feel bad. I even understand that. So, they might have considered old dad to be somewhat of a drag.

I am 77 now and retired, after surviving two different heart attacks and working for 30 years with the Veterans Administration. As part of my job I travelled. I was an Army veteran of the Viet Nam war, with a Purple Heart. Rose was a retired school teacher for the Princeton school system for 21 years. It seems that Rose was never ever sick.

We raised five children, two sons and three daughters. All are married and they have given Rose and me eight grandchildren. My son Marty is an FBI agent; Larry is an Air Marshall. My daughters Jill and Patty are stay-at-home mothers and Virginia is single and an attorney with a New York firm.

I have a great pension, and a VA disability check coming every month. Rose had a pension also, so financially we were alright. Rose and I invested in stock and we owned a few income properties, one of which was a house in Long Beach Island, where the entire family spent many great, wonderful days together. For many years, it was always wall-to-wall kids. our kids and some of their friend's kids in our house and at the beach.

Those days are now all over and are just the memories of an old man. I am happy that the kids now take turns using the beach house. Since we had retired, Rose and I loved to stay there in the off season in the fall and winter months when it was deserted. We both loved to walk on the beach at dawn, and when the sun set, we just sat and watched the sea.

Yes, I thought as I drove, this was going to be a great day. I was glad I did this. The sun was out and the sky was very blue with beautiful white clouds. I was now about to enter the Delaware Water Gap and both sides lining the road were filled with such beautiful colors. There was a slight chill in the air; "a little crispy" is what Rose would say.

I had booked a room until Monday at the lakeside resort that we loved. It was inexpensive and a wonderful place to just sit, to just rest, have a good meal and a great glass of wine and enjoy nature, the lake and the mountains. They offered a large glass-enclosed sun porch right off the dining room and bar area, overlooking the lake. One of the things we did was after dinner, like most folks, we would end up sitting in their wonderful rocking chairs and just sit and chat. The waitresses would keep coming to see that our glasses were always full. They had a large lake with a huge water fountain in the middle and at night when it got dark, they turned it on. It had multi-colored lights that flickered in the spray. It was gorgeous!

As I got closer to the resort, suddenly once again, I was so glad that I had decided to come. Because of Rose's passing, I had missed this for the last two years. As I turned off the highway and was driving up the long drive to the resort, I saw the lodge and thought, God, the colors of the leaves surrounding the buildings here are breathtaking.

It was about 3 in the afternoon when I checked in and I really smiled to myself as I was given room 316. Rose and I had that room many times. I remember it because of its great location away from the noise and its gorgeous views of both the lake and Mount Pocono.

Summer vacations were now over and the rooms were now filled with us foliage-crazy folks. I unpacked, laid down and took a nap. I was remembering our family vacations here.

It was about six when I dressed and went down to dinner. Tonight it was an Italian buffet. They had a large alpine dining room and the decor was outstanding: all hardwood floors and wood tables and chairs. They used a lot of white tablecloths and red napkins, and it somehow blended with the room. The food here always was wonderful and plentiful. However, I cannot eat as much now as I did when we first came here with the kids on vacation.

As I looked around, I noticed that there was not really a full house as it had been in the past. My server said that the economy was at fault this year. But it was still early and some folks arrived late. While I was eating, I made a call to my daughter to let them know that I was not at home, that I was here and safe.

Once more, I know they all loved and worried about me, but I got the usual "Dad, why don't you take someone with you?" or Marty said, "Dad, you shouldn't be alone. What if you fall? I'm worried about you."

All I knew was that for some reason I wanted to just get away; I knew that if I did tell someone they would have tried to talk me out of it. So I left without saying a thing. My usual routine was on Saturdays I usually go to my daughter Jill's house and see my three grandchildren. I love doing that; they are my life, what I now live for. But life goes on and kids grow. It was nice for us both when they were little, but now that they are getting bigger and they all have other interests and new things to do, they sit and talk to me for a while. Even though it's to be polite, they do for a while.

One of the things, when I get a chance, is that I start to tell them about things they should know, things that a grandfather should tell: family history and important family things. But I see that they have short attention spans and are not really interested, so then understandably they wander into another part of the house and do something or are on their computers. I end up sitting in a chair until it's time to leave.

Lately around my children and the family, I try be a happy dad, an up person. I put on and keep a happy face and appear happy, even though I am not.

Missing my love, my wife, is just something that never goes leaves me and never goes away. It's very, very hard to tell your children and make them understand just how God damn lonely I am without their mother. To me it is frustrating that no one understands. It's no one's fault, it simply is the way things are. Yes, lonely, that's what I am at this moment, lonely and sad, and I guess I spend time feeling a little sorry for myself.

Meeting Nick Rossi:

So I finished a great dinner and order a fresh glass of Chardonnay, then walk out to the porch. It had grown dark and the lights on the lake were lit. The large spraying fountain in the center of the lake constantly turned off and on and featured red, white, green, yellow and blue lights that were perfect and great in the water sprays. It was a beautiful sight.

In the darkness of the room, I saw a chair on the left side that was unoccupied at the time. It had a small table next to it, so I started to walk to it. When I reached there I suddenly noticed a white-haired man sitting on a bench to the right. At first he did not hear or see me. The lights from the lake were on his face, and his head was back. He was staring up into the heavens, and I could clearly see tons of tears were running down his face. He was not openly crying aloud, just slight tears.

Then he turned and quickly saw me and used his handkerchief to dry his tears.

I knew that I must had shocked him standing there and all I could say was "Are you, are you alright?" I asked.

"Oh," he said, surprised. "Oh, God, I'm sorry, I did not notice that anyone was watching me …. I just had one of the many relapses into my past, and the memory must have caused me to cry. Please, sir, sit."

"Sure, I understand, I think that you were…just remembering," I said. "Buddy, I think I know what you're thinking; your wife, right?"

"Yes," he said.

"Well, that's none of my business, my friend. I understand, because I've been there many times," I said as I sat down.

Then we both sat there not saying a word for at least 15 or 20 minutes

I notice that he was also sipping some wine. Since he was not talking, I thought about leaving him alone so he could be by himself and was about to do just that when he turned, looked at me, and asked, "How long has it been?"

"Been?" I asked, not understanding what he meant.

"How long ago did your wife pass?" he continued.

"Oh, two years, now."

"Oh, my wife passed a few years ago."

I looked out at the lake and I said to myself, this man still mourns after many years. He, like me, really must have loved her.

Another few minutes passed. There was just silence. We both were looking out at the lake.

A waitress came out and asked if we needed anything. We both told her that we were fine.

Then I said, "Rose, my wife and I, after the kids married and left home, would love to come here to see the autumn leaves……. She would collect a lot of leaves and she put them in books. They are still there in those books; you know…. just can't get myself to throw them out. She loved to collect four leaf clovers in the summer. So this morning, I thought I'd get away for a few days and relax."

"You sound like me,' he said, "except I am here with my daughter, her husband and my two granddaughters and their friends for four days. We just arrived today."

Then there was silence once more.

It was I who said, "My wife loved the food here, especially for some reason their breakfasts. We would get up early, walk all over the lake, head back and sit on the restaurant's patio outside tables and enjoy the early sun. My wife loved their blueberry pancakes."

"Yes. We also loved the breakfasts after our walk; sounds like we did the same things," he said. "By the way, my name is Nick Rossi."

I stood up, walked over, shook his hand, and said, "Nice to meet you, Nick. My name is Matt Mason." I said, "It's funny how we remember all those little things that didn't mean much before, but now we love to remember."

"Missing her today, huh?" he said, taking a sip and drying his eyes.

"Mmm, every day, it never ends," I replied.

"You said it had been two years since she passed, Matt, right?" he asked.

"Yes, almost two years," I said.

"I know it's so damn hard," he answered.

"Yes, that's what you said, today is very hard for me, too, Nick," I said. "I have such great memories, and all day long, I have been remembering many years ago. God! I think about when I first met her in a playground; we were just kids then. I don't know why, but early this morning as I was sleeping, it all came back to me. God, I could see her, Nick."

I was not really sure just why I was telling this man, a total stranger, this. But it felt so good talking to someone.

"I started to tell my children and grandkids about family things. Things that they really need to know, just yesterday morning, things she does not know, about her mom and I and how we first met…but I saw her eyes rolling back into her head. …Hum. Oh, well, kids think it is easy to forget and that I guess we older folks should get over it and go on with our lives," I said.

He laughed. "God! Do I know about that?"

"Yes, I know," I said. "I guess that's just life."

Then suddenly he sat straight up in his chair, turned to me and said, "Oh, God, I'm sorry, I'm shooting my mouth off …it's truly really great to hear someone share this with me. I'm in the same boat; got two children, both married and four grandkids. When I talk about my wife and our lives, they smile. I love them, but after a while, I know they don't hear me. I don't think they mean to, but I guess they also are tired of me and my stories of how it was. Sad, huh?" he said, looking out into space.

"Yes, Nick, my children too, it's true. Oh…of course I know that they miss and love their mother as all my kids do. One thing I remember from the past, in my life time growing up, things I heard my parents and many folks I knew and loved say about a guy like me and you, Nick: These were great wonderful, loving, sharing and caring folks, But, I remember hearing them say at one time or another when they saw someone going up the street whose loved one had died, they would say something like,'Oh, here comes so and so. They just lost their loved one. I love and feel sorry for him or her, but God, I wish they wouldn't stop in today; I am not in the mood today to be depressed'."

"Yes, I heard them and I understand what they meant. They were not being mean. But that's just how life is today; we don't want to hear other folk's troubles or see their tears. So…my friend, you and I are now one of those people they talked about. I tried hard to not tell anyone my thoughts and tried to smile," I said. "Nick, looks like we have to learn to handle our grief alone and keep our feelings inside. But is it so hard. I know for me it is; I don't know about you."

"You know, I don't ever remember having anyone explain it that way, Matt, but you are so right. Folks, they love you, but just don't want to hear it. I am so glad that I met you," he said.

Then I said, "I remember just last week with my grandchildren, I wanted to tell them, so they will know how we met, fell in love and married. But said they had to be someplace and they didn't want to talk then. I really felt a little bad then, because really I wanted them to know about their beautiful grandmom. I have so much, so much that I really want them to know. Little things. Things that made us love and stay together all these years. Throughout the good years and the not-too-good years, we bore it all together. But I guess I'll have to try to write it down sometime, hummm…..before it's too late," I said.

"God, Matt, you have no idea of tonight, in particular, I love talking to you. A few minutes ago, I was really down, and I was really depressed all day today. About to do something crazy, and then you, in just a few minutes, have made me feel so good," he said as he stood up.

"Look, I have to leave; I see my daughter and the family just arrived for dinner. We're having a late dinner. Are you going to be here for a few days? Look, Matt, I really would like to hear all about your life. You sound like a very interesting man. Maybe you will tell me more, tomorrow? Can you meet me tomorrow at 9 for breakfast? Please say yes!"

"Sure, Nick, I will be happy to meet you; I am retired with no place to go. I can stay as long as I want," I answered.

The Morning Breakfast:

It was early the next morning. I awoke early and took a walk, but it was just a short walk, not like we did when I was younger, but a nice walk in the brisk air. I arrived at the dining room at 9, found a table and ordered coffee, when I saw Nick arrive.

"Good morning, Matt," he said. "From my window I saw you taking a walk?"

"Yeah, but it was not a long one," I answered.

"Well, my legs won't allow me to walk too far any more. I brought my cane with me, just in case we might have to walk far," he said.

"Are you having breakfast?" I asked.

"Yes, coffee. I'm sorry that I invited you to breakfast, but at the time I did not know my daughter had made plans. My grandkids want to take me someplace; I don't know where. They plan to get something in a local restaurant that they all want to visit. But I wanted to stop and apologize, say good morning and once again tell you just how very, very much I enjoyed taking to you last night and to see if I can make it up to you by having dinner with me tonight, on me of course. It seems that they have a hay ride planned for this evening and that's not for me. Please, Matt, I really would like to talk more with you. Please, until last night it was hard for me to find anyone that understands and feels as I do. God. I'm being inconsiderate...I never thought... but it won't make you feel bad if I ask you to tell me more about your Rose, will it?" he asked.

"No, Nick, of course not," I said. I was really surprised that he wanted to hear about my life, but more than eager to tell him. "Have a great day with your family, Nick, and I would be honored to have dinner with you and talk. How about 7 o'clock? I will meet you in the lobby."

The Surprise Idea:

As I entered the lobby, I saw Nick out front of the building. He was standing by a car, helping his granddaughter into the back seat. He said good bye and came back in and waved.

"Just in time!" I said.

"Yes, they are all going on a hay ride and some kind of cookout after. We came here with my daughter's best friend and her husband and two kids and they want to do and see everything." he said. "Shall we?" he said, as he pointed to the dining room. "My son-in-law planned it and he is a great guy."

We had a wonderful, great dinner and he talked about all the things he did with his family today. It was curious to me that in our conversation he at three different times said the words when he talked about his life using the term "before it's too late."

All during dinner Nick kidded with our server, whose name was Nancy. Last night he looked so depressed but tonight he was funny and I know that she enjoyed us both.

"Look, Matt," he said as we finished, "you really don't know, but last night I enjoyed every single thing that you told me, so much that I thought about it as I slept last night. If you will, I would love to hear more. Now… Matt. this is going to sound absolutely crazy to you, I know; after all, we are complete strangers but I feel that we seem to both share a real need and desire to tell somebody, anybody, about our lives with our wives."

"Last night was one of my worst nights, but for some reason, after last night just hearing you, I could see that you also do not have anyone really interested in hearing your life story. So, I thought, since we are both here and we really do not know if we will ever have the real chance to tell our families what we really want they to know about our lives, and their mother, I wonder if you would be open to something. Again it might sound crazy."

"Would you be interested in you and I, while we are here, to just sit here? For us both to take our time and reminisce and recall everything we need and would want our families to know? For once to say it all, without any interruptions, and record it all on this tape I brought with me tonight?"

"Matt, I really would like to share my life with you as you share yours; does this sound too crazy to you? What I am suggesting is that I would like to record on tape our conversations about all that you are willing to tell me. Anything. ….. Let me finish before you answer. I propose that we each tell our story; just two old guys having a conversation here in the mountains. After we are finished, Matt, I will make copies for me and for you, and then, we can save them. And after we pass, maybe sometime in the future, if our children and grandchildren want, they can play these very tapes, play and hear our stories of the things that they need to know. They will be listening to our voices using our own words. They will have these tapes and hopefully they will see that our lives will be shared with our future relatives forever. Hearing these wonderful memories and things we both always wanted our families to know."

Matt, don't say no. Yes, it sounds crazy I know, but time is passing too fast for both of us. God only knows just how long you and I have. So, Matt, as crazy as it might seem, I thought that this opportunity might never come to you and me again. In this single recording, we can leave our kids something that I think is worth more than money: our recorded story."

I was shocked by his suggestion, but really intrigued by it all. I just looked at him for a few minutes. What harm would it do? I asked myself, then I said, "I would have never have thought of something like this."

"Is that a yes? Matt, is it alright with you? Now, I know we are complete strangers. I also realize that we are grown men. I guess grown men wouldn't do something like this. But for some reason, for once I would love to hear a truthful story of a man that really loved his wife as I did."

"That's my main point. For some reason I feel that you are not the ordinary guy, Matt, no, you are like me. Even though she is gone, you are still in love with her," he said, looking at me.

I, for some reason, loved the idea.

"Nick, I liked it. How did you come to think of it?" I asked.

"It was after our talk, I just felt from meeting you that we might do this. You will never know just how much I enjoyed our short conversation. We both need this. I know this is the time. For the very first time in my life, without any fear or caring who knows or hears this foolish old man's real story, I have a great desire, before it's too late for me, to share with someone (you, Matt!) those wonderful years and the exceptional life I had with this wonderful loving woman. I believe that you will also want to share yours, too. But look, yes I know it's nuts, but if you think it's weird, or something, then let's just forget it."

"I know that I am going on and on, but this is so damn important to me. You told me last night, the same thing: that even though they don't mean to, our families just really don't understand just how important it is to us that they know about our lives. I find it a little sad that we both have a wonderful story to tell and that simply no one wants to hear it. They are always just too busy and it seems they all have a short attention span when it comes to this. Yes, Matt, it is a sad thing and we have a chance to make it right. Otherwise, after you and I are gone, no one will ever know," he said.

I just looked at him; he was so very serious; I could see it clearly in his eyes. This meant so much to him. As he waited for my reply, I thought, yes, it was true that his request was very unusual and strange, but it also was very intriguing to me.

Again, it was something that I never would have thought of myself. It made more sense to me right now than it might have a few days ago. It would be a recorded history of my life with my bride, their mother. It was also true that this recording would have another person, a complete stranger, on it, too, a person each family would not know.

But the point of this all intrigued me, while we are having a conversation that is encouraging each of us to open up and tell as much as we could. I also thought that now that I thought it was a great idea, I could go home and do the very same thing myself with a tape recorder.

But I doubted if I would really do it, or if I did, would I say everything that needed to be said? So, like it or not, we two old guys have awakened the true essence of what we both feel our lives were, and to stop now could and would kill it forever. It was just a tape.

By this time and all though the day and at dinner I had consumed enough wine that I was in the mood to honor his request to at least try it. So we walked out on the porch, chatted a little longer and drank some more wine.

I told him that I would be honored to do this with him, and that I loved the idea.

I saw a light twinkle in his eyes and a broad smile on his face. It was clear to me that this was very important to him.

Telling My Story:

Finally, he suggested, "Let's get started. How did you first meet Rose?"

I sat back, closed my eyes, and started.

"Well, to really explain, I have to go back. The first time I ever saw Rose, I was 13 years of age and playing baseball sponsored by a local realtor. We had just finished the game. I was walking home from the field with my friends, when we stopped at a new playground that just openned in a new housing project in our area called The Rogers Homes."

"These were three story all brick apartment houses with a total of 27 units in each building. They were being constructed for the deserving veterans with families. After the war there was a great shortage of homes for the veterans; many had war brides. Each day more and more families moved in and more and more new kids with them. So this playground was made for them. I'm sure you remember that time. At that time, I was a pure boy, into only sports and eating."

"I spotted this redheaded young girl walking to the swings. She was wearing a white blouse and kelly green shorts. Up until then girls never interested me. Seeing her, I went and sat at one of the tables with some kids I knew. They were talking to me, but I did not hear them because all the time, I was watching her."

"God, she was beautiful. I knew many girls, some very pretty, but never like this. I sat there talking for at least an hour, and all the time I was watching her and what she did. She was on the swings, then to a table talking to some other girls. I still had my eyes on her. Soon I had to leave."

"I did not see her for another few weeks; this time in was in the corner convenience store. She was wearing yellow shorts. I asked a friend that lived near her and he told me her name was Rose Tozzi; she was 12 and her dad was Mike Tozzi. He was the barber who had a shop on Maple Street. She was in the 8th grade at the local junior high school. He said that he did talk to her and that she was very nice."

"Since it was in July, I knew that in September, when school opened, she and I would be in the same 8th grade. And we were. Now, at this age, as far as girls go, Nick, I was a real ass, a jerk. I soon discovered that I was so shy and even at times petrified of girls. After a while, around the other kids, of course I got to know and talk to her, but nothing cool. She did not seem to care or even notice me and that really bothered me. Somehow I had the feeling that she didn't like me at all. But still I watched her, in class, in the school yard, walking home and around the neighborhood."

"Now, Nick, I got to stop here and tell you something that I have told folks, even my kids over hundreds of times. Rose was always so beautiful and to this day, I truly don't believe she really ever knew just how beautiful she was, even at age 71 when she passed."

"Came November, and the kids' weekend routine was Friday night to a local dance. There were places to dance all over town. Sundays was to the movies. My gang always went to the dances in the projects which were called 'The Homes' but I found out that Rose went to a local church's dances on Friday, where I had never been before."

"A full year would go by. I really thought I never would have a chance, even that she was really too good for me. So I just drifted though the next few months."

"I was now sixteen, and one Friday they canceled our dance. I remember the church where Rose would be at, hopefully, so I went, alone. It's funny now to remember, Nick, it had to be the same in your neighborhood. It seems all the boys were on one side of the room and the girls on the other, like fish in a pond. Girls mostly danced with other girls. I watched as boy after boy went over and asked her to dance and she did. I saw then just how popular she was. Like I said she was gorgeous."

"I guess that watching all this convinced me that I was wasting my time; I was, I guess, jealous. I didn't know why, after all I was always a popular kid, but when it came to girls, especially her, I discovered that I had very low personal esteem. Frustrated, I realized it was getting late. I was about to leave and go to the Ewing Diner where everybody met after all the dances."

"I was sitting there and she walked over to me, looked at me, and said, 'Are you ever going to ask me to dance?' I was floored; I never expected that, no way! We started to dance and lord knows I was not too good a dancer to begin with and on top of that I was shaking and nervous. I didn't know just how to hold a girl, where to put my hands, God, didn't know what to say. I know my face had to be red. We were dancing to the record 'Sixteen Candles' and I tried not to get too close. Like I said, I was very nervous at first as we danced. I didn't know just how to hold her or what to talk about."

"We danced together the rest of the night. Soon, I think she sensed my problem and helped me. She talked to me about things that I could talk about. She smiled and I guess she felt good. She seemed to like me a lot and in small ways, in just a few hours, made me sense that. She even told me that I was a good dancer."

"I was in heaven! From the first night with her, I learned that Rose was so affectionate and she would be that way all our lives. After the dance as usual all the gang went to the Ewing Diner for Cokes and hamburgers. During the last dance, somehow I got it out and asked if she was going there. I wanted to see if I could see her again. She said that she would meet me there."

"Since I didn't drive, we all got around in our friend Ronnie's car. He was 17. So Ronnie drove us to the diner. There were all the kids from this dance and other dances in the community. It seems that we all somehow, whatever dance you went to, all in the end came here. The owner of the diner's name was Gus and he was a great guy. His waitresses were some of the kid's mothers and grandmothers. It was a great place to go. We all made sure that we behaved ourselves out of respect."

"I saw that Rose was already there when I entered. She was in the back booth sitting with three other girls and it was plain to me that she and her friends were waiting for me to enter the door. It seems her girlfriends were kidding her. I heard, 'Rose has a boyfriend,' from one of them and I heard Rose say, 'Shut up, Terry!'

"I blushed; I waved at her. I was so happy, because what Terry had said in a sense told me what I wanted and was happy to know. Simply, that Rose liked me; that itself seemed to take away the nervousness and the fear of rejection that all young boys had at that time."

"It was crowded and I sat on the stools opposite their booth and talked with Rose. Terry was just looking at me and smiling. I said to Rose, 'Are you finished? Let's go outside,' and we did. We walked over and both leaned on Ronnie's car and just talked small stuff, like about school and other things. Most kids that were 'going together' would just talk in the parking lot, so everyone saw us. My buddies and her friends of course were peeking out the windows at us. We talked until Ronnie came and wanted to leave. Ronnie lived on the same block as Rose and they talked just bit."

"Before we left, I walked over and said, 'Rose, when can I see you again?' She said, 'Call me tomorrow' and she gave me a paper with her telephone number on it."

"'Sure,' I said and got into Ronnie's car. On the way home, the guys were kidding me, but they were also very envious of me because Rose was beautiful, friendly and a nice person. 'You're lucky, jerk,' Ronnie said, as I got out of his car in front of my house."

"And that, Nick, was how Rose and I first met."

Then I said, "Nick, is this what you want? God, I have so much to say. Maybe I am telling too much, too descriptive... it's going to take a lot of tape."

"Oh, no, Matt, that was so great. The way you described it all, hell, I thought I was there with you. That is exactly what I want. Did it make you feel good, Matt, telling me, a stranger, and getting all of that out? And Matt, when was the last time to you told anyone that story?" he said, looking at me.

"Never ! I never did, but I wanted to, tried to tell the kids. But..... Anyway, yes, I felt good telling you that. What great memories!" I said.

25

"You want to stop now?" Nick asked.

"No," I said.

"Then please continue; I love hearing about your life," Nick said, sitting back in his chair again. "Take all the time you want and, Matt, you tell me just want you want me to know. I tell you that this is important to us both."

"OK. I called Rose the next day and we talked for hours. I asked her to go to the movies and we did. She was so much fun and had a wonderful laugh. Again, she was so affectionate- wanting to hold hands all the time: in the movies, walking outside, in the diner or wherever. Rose would look at me, and with her hand she would brush my hair back, straighten my ties, and do things like that."

Meeting The Family:

"After that, we started to date. I was invited over one Sunday to her grandmother's house after church for Sunday breakfast. Rose said that this was a big usual thing with her grandmother. She had a large house, with an enormous sun room. I learned that all her children and their children and other relatives came over about 11 every Sunday morning and had breakfast with each other. This had been going on for a long time, and it was a way that they helped keep the family together. Each family would bring something; the women would cook eggs, bacon, sausages and other things. This was a big thing: I was going to meet that whole family!"

"Her house was outside of town and was like an old farm house. When I pulled in the driveway, Rose came out to meet me. I was dressed in dress pants, a blue shirt and looked good. Rose hugged me, kissed my cheek, squeezed my hand and said, 'Don't be nervous. These are nice people; you're going to love them.' "

"As we walked in the door, her father and mother came over. Her father was a big man. He shook my hand and simply said, 'Welcome,' with a smile. Her mother both hugged me and kissed my cheek. Then I heard Grandma Millie say as she entered coming from the kitchen (and what she said I loved and still love it. It kind of broke the ice, at least for me), 'Where's my Rosie's dream boat?' "

"Rose hollered, 'Grandma!' "

"'What?' she said. 'Come here, Matt. Hmmm. Turn around, let me take a peep at your boy, …Rosie, he looks like a dream boat to me…If you don't want him, some girl is going to snatch him from you!' and she laughed and hugged me tight."

" 'Ma! Stop it; you're embarrassing the boy,' her father said. 'Come over here and sit, Matt,' he said, pointing to a picnic table. That morning I met the family. She had a sister Anna and a brother Paul. I met uncles, aunts, nieces and nephews and many old family friends. Her grandfather had died a few years back. It was a great day and they all made me feel so welcomed.'"

"I would attend three more of these breakfasts, when her dad and his brother Frank and Grandma came over to the table where I was sitting and her father said, "Matt, we want to ask you something. You have had breakfast here a few times now.' Then Frank said, 'Yeah, we would like to know if there is something we have for breakfast you would like to eat that we don't serve now.' "

"I was confused and I said, 'I love your food.' "

"Yeah, but there must be something you would like besides; think of something,' " her dad added."

I thought for a minute, seeing that now everyone in the room was looking at me. I knew they wanted me to say something so I said, 'Cream puffs.' "

"With that, Grandma said, 'O.K., cream puffs it is. Matt, you are now in charge of bringing cream puffs. How's that everyone? Matt is our cream puff guy. Matt, you stop at the Paramount Bakery just down the street each week and just pick them up. Tell Margie I sent you. We will pay for them; you just see that you bring them here. You are our cream puff guy!'"

"With that, everyone laughed, and Rose threw her arms around me and whispered in my ear, 'My family has just voted you into our family, Matt. You are our official cream puff guy; you now have to bring a dozen cream puffs when you come. I love you!'"

"Then they started to invite my mom and dad to their gatherings. I was loved, I know, by this wonderful family, and I attended many, many of her family's houses all over for different occasions. The Sunday suppers with an Italian family at that time was unbelievable. All the food, and I never saw so many friends, family and relatives in one house. You could not get them all in the dining room."

"So, the next few months were wonderful. Rose and I were inseparable. I will always remember one little thing, that was that Rose loved to hold my hand. When I bought my first car, a Plymouth yellow convertible, when we drove, she would sit close and when we walked, sat or did anything, whenever she could, she would find my hand and hold it. I just loved that."

The Viet Nam War:

"Then my life got a little stupid and messed up, because I had made a bad decision. One year before, when I was seventeen, Rose's older brother Paul, who soon became my best friend, invited me to join the National Guard unit that he belonged to. He was 17 and my birthday was close. He took me up to the Armory and gave me a tour. As I was about to graduate from high school and going to enroll in our community college, I did not want to join, so I just told Paul that I would think about it. But I never did, and then as my luck would have it, the Vietnam War started. In the next year I would be eighteen and at draft age. To stay out of the possible draft, I was warned by Paul to join the National Guard. I didn't want to; I wanted college. But against all hope a year later I received my draft notice and it was too late for me to act."

"So, I was drafted. Of course it was a shock to all of us. No one ever said, but I knew many thought that I should have joined the National Guard when I could have. I never dreamed this could really happen to me and I did not want to go, but there was nothing I could do. This was all my own fault. Rose was sad and so was my family. But I said to all of them that they would see that the months would fly by and I would be back. I was sent to Fort Dix, NJ, for training and then it seemed in no time I was deployed. I got a pass and I went home to be with my family before leaving."

"Look, Nick, I really don't want to talk about a lot of this part. It was so hard; this was an unpopular war and many guys were going to Canada. This was mentioned and suggested to me and to tell you the truth, I thought hard on it. But I couldn't do such a thing, so I reported back. I have to tell this in our recording. It was a very, very terrible and hard thing to do to leave our loved ones. I hurt when I remember, so I won't talk about the parting."

"Although it is all like a dream to me now, traveling and arriving there. I really don't like to remember any of this. But I have to tell you this, because what I am going to remember and tell you, I have never revealed to my children, nor anyone."

Getting Attacked:

"I was deployed and was there for 11 months; the weather was rotten. My unit had been out in the field for three days. It was so cold there that morning, they sent us in to a field mess tent for some hot chow and rest."

"My buddy, Tommy Hubbard, from Jessup, Georgia, and I and our SSgt Clark found a shady spot under the large tent and near a stove to get a little warm. We were sitting on some metal containers that had held food at one time. We were just talking when I decided that I wanted more coffee, so with my mess kit cup, I stood up and started to walk over to the other side to get some. Just then, there was that noise of an unexpected massive shelling all around us and we were also being attacked with small arms. Then all Hell broke loose; suddenly, with many explosions. I was knocked to the ground by an explosion and I felt pain in my right leg, my left arm and my stomach. I had been hit by a machine gun of some kind. I rolled myself up in a ball, rolled over, got my weapon and started to return fire. I know I hit at least three who were running back into the forest. It all lasted only a few minutes."

"I then heard a lot of screaming. I turned around fast and I saw that the tent Tommy and I were sitting under was now completely ablaze. I saw SSgt Clark was beneath the burning tent and he was trying to get it off him, but I didn't see Tommy. I then saw a long rope hanging that was attached to the end of the tent; it was not far from me. I was hurting and bleeding but somehow I crawled over as far as I could. I got up and grabbed the rope and pulled it with all I could, and it pulled the tent off him. When I did that, I saw Tommy had been under that tent. When I tugged on it once more, Tommy was free of it, but he was on the ground; his back was on fire. I saw two guys start rolling him in the dirt and throwing dirt on him trying to put it out. The last thing I saw was that those guys had gotten to him and put the fire out."

"I must have passed out; because when I awoke I was in a hospital tent. I was in pain; I was told that my right leg was broken, my left arm also, and that I had six pieces of steel in my body. I was in pain and drifted in and out for two days. When I finally awoke I asked about Paul and SSgt Clark. I could not get an answer; no one could tell me anything. It took a few days, but my Company Commander came and told me that SSgt Clark had managed to live for a week, but he suffered a lot of small arms fire and then died from his wounds. He said that Tommy was burnt pretty badly, he did not know how badly, but they flew him to a hospital ship and he was in a burn center. He said we lost two others besides SSgt Clark for a total of 3 that day, and we killed 9 and captured 2."

"He said that he had no idea just how the enemy got though our protected lines. I at that time was not interested and heard little he said after that. This had been my worst fear and it happened. I lived through it, but I lost three great friends. I will never in my life forget SSgt Clark. There, I told you all of that, Nick... Didn't really want to remember or tell this but I guess it has to be known."

"I was taken to Army Hospital where they operated and removed the bullets and some pieces of steel. My leg had been broken in the blast and I had to have a steel rod and some screws. I possibly might walk with a limp as a result. My arm healed very well. They had discovered that from the blast, I had lost some of my hearing for a long while, but since then it has improved. They were going to release me, but I had to go to a VA hospital for some more treatments."

"All that time. I could only get to call home a few times. The hospital was just too far for anyone to come see me and I was kind of discouraged by that. When I could, I got to call my mom and dad and Rose three or four times. We wrote letters back and forth. Boy. If we only had the cell phones we had today. But, that's a different story."

"Before I left, I discovered that Tommy had bad burns on his right side, his back, right arm and leg and part of his face. He had taken some of that steel in his back near his spine and he also suffered second and third degree burns. The second degree burns on his back and legs healed within a month; however, the third degree burns on his arm, neck and face would need years of skin grafting. He had had two operations on his back and there were to be more. His burns would heal and he might be scarred in different places for life."

"I called his dad, who told me that Tommy was very depressed and the doctors were doing their best to help him. He was taken to the burn center hospital in Georgia. He promised to keep me posted. I told his dad that as soon as I could I would try to visit. However, Tommy was to pass away in his sleep a few months later at home. His dad said it was from complications from his wounds. He said that Tommy always wanted to be cremated and they were doing that soon."

Coming Home:

"I was so depressed for a few weeks; the doctors came and talked to me. I knew that I was never going to get over this. Then they gave me my orders to come home. So, only calling my dad and mom, I told them and asked that they tell no one. I wanted this is to be a surprise. Before I was discharged, I was awarded a Purple Heart by a Major who told me that I might receive more. They arranged my flight into Newark, NJ, and I called my mom and dad to meet me at the airport."

"As soon as I reached them, coming off the plane, Mom crying and Dad hugging me had the passageway stopped. There were folks behind us also anxious to get off the plane. They smiled, understood why they were made to stop for a few minutes, but were patient until we moved out of the way."

"We went over to the benches in the airport. My mom and dad sitting and holding me on both sides of me just cried and cried and squeezed the Hell out of me. We had to wait because the airport provided a wheel-chair to the car. My mom sat in the back with me and continued to cry until I got her calmed down."

"As we approached my town, seeing those wonderful buildings, the church, the high school and a sweet shop along the way, I could not help it, but tears of joy just filled my eyes and rolled down my face. I am home,

I thought to myself. Yes, I cried too. There were times I thought I would never see this town again; it looks so good to me."

"My family just wanted to take me right home, where they had arranged a bed on the first floor for me. But I told them no, that I just had to, just HAD to see Rose and her family. I was going to surprise them; I had waited too long."

Now my mom and dad loved me; I knew that it had been such a long flight that I might be too tired, that they really wanted me to rest and thought that the family could come to our home later that day. But I had been thinking of Rose all the time, every day, it seems every hour since I left. God, in the hospital and on the flight home, I kept dreaming over and over of meeting Rose and her mom and dad today so I insisted to them that I wanted to see them first. I needed to. My dad understood, but Mom, being Mom, worried that it may be too hard on me."

"As we turned into her street, they did not know that I was coming. I saw Rose and her grandma taking bags of food out of the trunk of the car, putting them on the porch. My dad began to honk the horn and wave his hand shouting, "Rose, Rose look who is here!"

"She stopped, turned around and looked, with her mouth wide open. Rose saw me in the back and she sprang to the car before it stopped, trying to open the door before Dad could stop. She came screaming my name out loud, so hard, that neighbors looked our way. She was waving her hands in the air, screaming. She ran to the rear door where I was and she opened it, desperately reaching for me. She was screaming; slowly somehow I got out and stood up as she squeezed me and held me and held me and cried and cried. She was crying and saying things I could not understand; she kissed me over and over again. There were tears flowing and streaming down her face. She was breathing so hard it was scaring me, and crying so hard it was hard for her to talk and say anything."

"Of course I was crying like a baby. I hadn't planned to, I didn't want to, but my emotions of coming home, seeing the town I might not have ever seen again, seeing my family and now Rose, why, I was just overwhelmed by it all and I had absolutely no control whatsoever over my emotions. Finally, Grandma came, actually gently pulled Rose off me and helped me stand up. Dad handed me my cane. Grandma was very emotional, too; she wiped her eyes and said, 'Let's all go inside.'"

"As I started to walk, Rose on one side and Mom on the other, I saw that it seemed that all the neighbors were now out and watching this entire reunion. I saw the folks that I knew before I left, both men and women, with tears in their eyes. I waved at them; I still could not talk. They all just clapped. Grandma led us all into the house. She led us to the back sun room, then helped me to my favorite chair and helped me sit. Rose sat on the floor next to me, holding my hand."

"It was less than a half hour later when I heard the front door bang and the sound of folks running, then Rose's mom and dad, her sister Anna and her Uncle Frank came running into the room. 'Mr Ross from across the street called and told us you were here, Matt! What a wonderful surprise; God bless that you are now safe,' Rose's mother said, as she went behind my chair, kissed the top of my head, and hugged me. Her dad and Uncle Frank were so emotional. Her sister Anna just kissed me and sat on the floor before my feet."

"I was now so overcome with emotion. I had thought of my homecoming all the time that I was hospitalized. I was openly a total mess and crying out loud and saying, 'Oh my God, Oh my God, ---I am so glad to see all of you. You have no idea just how much I missed you all. I don't know what to say. You all look so damn good!' "

"Then I looked at Rose, sitting on the floor in front of me with tears in her eyes, yet with a smile that I had waited so long to see. 'Rose, every minute of my days I thought of you. When I was hit, I thought of you; when I woke up in the hospital, I thought of you; as I worked hard to get better, and on the way home, I thought of you. Promise that you will never let me leave you again. Baby I love you so damn much it hurts me,' I said, pulling her up to sit on my lap as I kissed her."

Asking The Question:

"She was about to answer when her brother Paul rushed into the room and, without looking, running towards me he slipped on a throw rug and slid up to Anna on the floor before me. We all laughed. He got up on his knees before me and hugged the Hell out of me. I pushed Paul aside and said, 'Wait, wait, wait, Paul. I was about to ask your sister something.' They all looked at me as I was still torn up by this homecoming. They wondered what I was going to ask."

"I took Rose's hand, looked at her in the eyes and said, 'Rose, I had to come here first because before this day is over I have to ask you something. I have practiced this over a million times, when I was getting ready to ask you before, and just when Paul came. I can't stand to wait any longer. Rose, you have been in my mind every minute since I left you. Every day wherever I was or whatever I was doing, I thought of you. It is also so true that I thought of you when I woke up in the hospital. All those days of recuperating, I thought of you. I thought of you on the plane here, in my father's car and today when I saw your face again. Promise that you will never let me leave you again, baby. I love you so damn much it hurts me.' "

"'So today, right now, here before all our families, I ask you, Rose, God, God! Rose, I waited so long to ask you and again, I think that this is the time and the right place. Will you marry me; will you be my wife?' "

"With that I pulled out the ring I had bought in Japan and held it out to her. I knew that no one was expecting this. It was a surprise, especially to Rose. Rose looked at me, took the ring in her hand then put her hands on both sides of my faces and looked in my eyes with the love that I somehow always knew was there. She cried as she repeated saying, 'yes, yes, yes' over and over again. She kissed me and held me so close. I heard everyone talking or saying something but they all could have been a million miles away because all I saw was Rose."

"Nick, I had survived and returned home safe, and now I had finally asked the question I wanted to for so long. I was so happy; I kissed and held her on my lap for what seemed to be hours. Neither Rose nor I felt the hands of our loved ones that were touching us. When I became focused again, I saw my mother and Roses' mother hugging in front of us. My father was behind me, and I could both feel and hear his cries of joy for us. Paul and Anna were standing there because they could not get close to us."

"That is how, Nick, I really asked my wife to marry me. I have never told anyone all of this before. I tear up when I remember."

"I was to spend some more time in a VA Hospital. It deeply hurt me because each time I went, I was one of many veterans spat upon and harassed by folks that hated the war. I was not to be seen in my uniform, or I would be spat upon and called many names. This hurt me a lot. I would walk with a limp with the steel rod and screws in my leg. I had some slight hearing loss in my right ear.

A Surprise Award:

Two months later I was very surprised and very proud that I was notified that I was going to be awarded the Army's Distinguished Service Cross along with the Purple Heart I had been given. It was for bravery under fire and other things like that. It was awarded at a ceremony at Fort Dix, NJ, with other veterans that my family and friends attended. The protesters were screaming outside."

"God, just remembering hurts me. Let's stop this now, Nick. I've said enough. Please shut it off."

Nick looked me and shut the recorder off until I could get myself together.

"OK, if you want, Matt. That was some story, Matt. Very interesting, powerful and so wonderfully emotional," he said. "Did you get married right after that?"

"Turn it back on," I said.

"Yes, Nick. We had a very big wedding; our mothers saw to that. We went on our honeymoon to Hawaii and loved it there. We bought a house in West Windsor, NJ, near Princeton."

"It was not long before my son Marty was born, then Jill, Patricia, and Lawrence. The last was Virginia. Rose stayed home for three years but then she wanted to get back to work. She taught in the Princeton school system for many years while I finished getting my college degree."

"While still going to college, I was working for the Veterans Administration. Life was great. It seems our life was so great: we did so many things with the kids, we traveled, and we were there for all the soccer games, baseball, football, and dance recitals. We saw them through the crazy teen years and we watched them grow into adults."

"Rose and I had always wanted to travel. While it was true that I had heart problems and a bum leg from the war, we not going the let that stop us. We were planning to visit relatives and friends for a few months and then take a sightseeing train ride across the US along the Canadian border, then end up in Vancouver and head down to San Diego to visit an old army buddy for a week and then fly home."

"But then, it was on a Sunday, four years ago now, Jill and the grandchildren were over at our house and it seemed that Rose could not get up from the couch. She had some pain. She tried, but we decided to take her to the hospital. I thought she had a back spasm, that they would give her a muscle relaxer and send her home."

"But it was worse than we had imagined. Rose, it seems, had stage four cancer. It started in her left breast and went into her spine. How could this happen? Did Rose know? Anyway it was a shock to us all. They started treatments at once. They tried them all. Radiation and all other kinds. At first she was cheerful. Then we were told it was spreading rapidly and was in her liver."

"We were told that there was no hope. They suggested we take her to hospice, since we were living alone, so that they could provide a caring environment and take care of her physical and emotional needs."

"This hit me so bad and it was happening so fast, Nick, I was going crazy. But I had to hold it together for her and the family's sake. Rose was told and accepted it. Alone I told her that I wanted to take her home. She smiled and said, 'Yes, take me home, Matt.' "

"My children thought it might be a bad idea because of my heart, but I didn't care; I have been to those hospices and they are very cold. I did not want my wife to be awaking in a strange place with no family."

"I arranged for a hospital bed to be delivered to my house the next day, and they brought her home. I had a visiting hospice nurse come. I could not and still cannot believe just how Rose handled this. She was so brave and at peace. The visiting nurses at first came daily until Rose grew worse, then it was around the clock."

"Alone with her at night, I talked to her and we remembered things. She asked me to do a few things after she was gone, and told me to take care of myself, because the children were going to need me now more than ever. I promised."

"She got weaker and weaker. Two nights somehow I managed to lay next to her holding her and thereafter I spent the rest of the nights in a chair near her bed holding her hand. The nurses were great, kind and caring and they understood that I constantly needed to be next to her."

"All the children and grandchildren came and said their goodbyes. Rose, by this time, constantly just faded in and out. The pain medicine needs grew more and more. Rose seemed to hear the words as each person said, 'I love you,' and even with her eyes closed, very faintly she managed to say to each somehow 'I love you, too.' "

"Rose lasted 44 days since she had gone to the hospital. We were all there with her when the end came. The priest had given her the last rites. She just closed her beautiful eyes and was gone from me. Gone from me forever. We all cried and each went to the bed, said goodbye and left. She died about three o'clock in the morning."

"My sons stayed and Virginia called the funeral parlor. They came, but I just could not be there when they took her away, Nick."

With that, I started to cry.

"We need to stop now Matt," Nick said, wrapping his arms around me.

"Nick. Thanks. You too. Leave me here. I will be OK. I need to be alone now," I said.

"Are you sure, Matt?" he asked.

"Yes, yes, Nick. Please just let me be," I said.

"OK," he said, and he shut off the recorder.

"Yes, Nick lets finish this later. I still want to hear your story," I said, trying to get myself in order.

"Will you be OK? Think I can I tell you after breakfast tomorrow; we don't have a lot of time to finish this," Nick said.

"Ok, then we will do as much as we can then," I said as I started to walk slowly towards the lobby to get a drink and be alone.

Recording Nick's Story:

That night, as I lay thinking about all of what I told the recorder, I had a very hard time trying to sleep. It had been very highly emotional experience for me. I guess I realized for the first time just how unusual but just how valuable these tapes were really going to be. I had opened my heart and told it all, and lying here, reliving now what I said, I knew that what I told him were the most precious the things I remembered. I did not believe that not once, not at any time in a real setting with one or any of my children, that I could have expressed this story so well. This was going to be a great blessing for Nick and myself.

The next morning after breakfast, Nick was very concerned about me. I assured him that I was fine and told him my thoughts on these talks. Nick, being concerned for me, suggested that we stop. "No!" I said, "I think this is a great idea. I told Nick that he and I feel that we both really want and need this, so let's continue.

Nick quickly agreed and then said he found a quiet section of the grounds, where he had the crew put two comfortable chairs and a table for them to sit and where they would not be disturbed.

Nick also got the kitchen to give him a large container of coffee that keeps it hot, cups, milk and some sweet rolls, and put them on a table for them.

"I told them we were businessmen talking business," he said.

When we were both comfortable, Nick turned on the recorder and started his story.

"Matt, all last night I was remembering your story; that was a great story. I thank you for sharing it with me. I knew it took a lot out of you. God, your story should be a movie. I could both see and feel the love you had for Rose. God bless you for sharing."

"Nick, you are going to make me cry, buddy. I have been waiting to hear your story. Tell me it all, all of it; we have plenty of time so don't miss a thing," I said, reaching over and touching his hand."

"OK, Matt…I would love to tell you how I first met. I grew up in Bronx, New York, in a place in my town known as 'Little Italy.' There were deli's, bakeries, cafes, restaurants and all types of businesses. My dad and his brother had an Italian restaurant, Rossi's Villa, my family from my grandfather, his brothers, and his sons. There were Rossi's family restaurants in North New Jersey and in New York City. The family also had two concessions for over 25 years at the Jersey Shore boardwalks in the summer. One was in Seaside Park and the big one, a few steps from the Steel Pier in Atlantic City. These were popular and very profitable for the entire family. We all shared working there."

"I worked since I was a kid in my father's place, not as a cook, but helping prepare, bus boy, dish washer and odd jobs. I sometimes delivered in the neighborhood, but walking distance as I could not drive yet; I was 15. That's when I first saw my wife."

"Just down the street from our place there was an all-girl Catholic school, Saint Pauline Catholic Church. There were quite a few Catholic schools in the neighborhood. I went to the other Catholic school. For a long while, for years this area had been filled with all Italian families coming from the old country. Then slowly a lot of Irish and Polish families started to move in. You know that old tradition that Italians marry only Italians, that Irish girls don't date or marry Italians or Polish boys, and of course those old taboos were giving way to the more modern ways after the World War."

"It was a Friday; I was getting ready to go to Atlantic City with Uncle Sal next weekend for a week on the boardwalk. I was crossing the street and three girls in uniform were crossing from the other side. I saw this beautiful blonde girl with a smile that caught my eye. They walked passed me, all saying, "Hi," and I turned to follow that girl."

"They all went into Chris's Sweet Shop. I stood there for a minute. My dad owned a restaurant across the street and of course every day I saw girls. Sharp and very pretty girls and all seemed to flirt with me through the window. I had no problem at all with girls. But there was this one girl…. I don't know, there was just something about her. You bet I knew she was Irish, you could tell."

"It was about a week later, I saw her going to the bus stop, so I was walking fast because school was over. This was the last day and I knew I might not see her for a while. This was the weekend I had to get to know her. She had on a pure white shirt and a blue dress. She was a knock out. She was sitting on a bus stop bench. I guess she was going somewhere. I walked over and said, 'Hi, I'm Nick Rossi.' "

"She looked up smiled and said, "\'My name is Barbara Kelly.'

" 'I've seen you walk by here a few times,' I said.'

" 'Yeah, I remember,' she said, moving over on the bench as if telling me to sit down, which I did. 'You're the family from Rossi's Villa up the street.' "

" 'Yeah, my dad owns it; ever go there?' I asked.'"

" 'Yes, with my grandfather and my family a few times, but it was always at night for the summer. My grandfather is a policeman; my dad is a fireman. I think my grandfather knows a lot of your family. He loves your food,' she said with a smile. 'Most of my family are policemen, except my dad and my Uncle Tommy; they are firemen. My dad is right over there,' and she pointed to the firehouse on the next block.

"Just then, the bus was pulling in and she saw it and got up."

" 'I'm going away down the shore with some of my family for a week. Will I see you again?" she asked."

"Then as I did sometimes, I asked a stupid question. 'Do you want to see me again?' "

"With that she just smiled and got on the bus. I sat there as the bus pulled away. I found out that she was also 15 and had two brothers who were older than she was: Joe and Patrick. Patrick was a student at CUNY and wanted to be a lawyer. One thing the guy told me was that Patrick did not like Italians at all and because his family were New York firemen and cops he just liked to pick fights most times over nothing."

"I needed a way to her see this summer. I knew who to ask, but I was leaving in the morning with my cousins for Atlantic City. It was start of the season, time for all the kids in all the Rossi family to get ready for the family's summer shore season. Every year, all the kids of our large family would all go to work at one of the seashore concessions. We all would rotate to whichever place where we were needed."

"This year I was going to help out in Atlantic City. I loved that; it was across from the Steel Pier. We were always busy there and sold hundreds of sandwiches there in a day. We would start real early in the morning getting ready for the rush."

"All this is important because of a hand of faith, that God must have planned happened to bring Barbara and me together once more."

"It only happens like this in a movie. It was early Monday morning, around 6:30 AM. Uncle Sal and I and my cousin Vincent were there on the boardwalk. We had to get things ready for the day. We were setting up and getting the onions and peppers cooked. Uncle Sal asked me to help him bring the trash in the back. We were doing that when we heard a fight of some kind. It was down the block just off the boardwalk in a secluded spot. Sal and I ran there and we saw three grown men, one with the top of a trash can and one with baseball bat, and they had a young guy on the ground."

"The guy with the bat was hollering, 'What do you want here, asshole. Did you see anything?' "

"The guy on the ground kept saying, " 'Nothing! Man, I don't know what you are talking about; I was just walking the boardwalk.' "

"Sal saw that the guy with the baseball bat was going to strike this guy. Now my Uncle Sal was a very big man and had no fear of anything, so he immediately jumped off the boardwalk into the sand and shouted to this stunned crew, 'You hit that guy and you are a dead man!' I ran right to his side and I still had the large butcher knife we used to cut peppers in my hand. These guys looked and acted as if they were drunk."

"When I tell you that Uncle Sal scared the shit out of these three guys, believe me, he did. They slowly backed off and got back on the boardwalk, telling Uncle Sal that they had no quarrel with him. Uncle Sal said nothing, just gave them all his look and with his arm he pointed down the boardwalk and in a flash they were gone."

"We went to the guy; it seems that when he fell, his right hip landed on a broken bottle. His hand was bleeding not a lot, but not as bad as his right hand was. So Sal told him to go around the back and come into our kitchen. Sal called the police,; they were there fast but could not find those guys."

"Then Uncle Sal got out the first aid kit for the guy's hand. He told the guy that the police were coming and sending an ambulance. We asked what happened and he said that he was just walking on the boardwalk and they just came out of nowhere. They thought he saw something. He then told Sal that he and his family came down from New York and had just arrived last night for a week's vacation. As he was taking an early walk, they jumped him from the street side of the boardwalk, shouting and wanting to know what he saw and why he was there. We gave him some coffee I had just made for him and we waited for the police."

"Then Sal shouted for Vincent and me to get back to work so we started once again to prepare for the day. I was cutting the peppers and onions when the cops came and I was sitting at the work station right near them as they talked. That's when I heard him say that his name was Patrick Kelly, that he was from New York and that his family were all cops."

"I said to myself, 'Could this be Barbara's brother? How could that be? So far from home and I would meet him here, like this?' I thought that there had to be a mistake, but Uncle Sal said, 'Hey. You have an Uncle Timmy Kelly, a fireman?' to which he answered, 'Yeah, why?' Uncle Sal then said, 'Son of a bitch. You're kidding man; he's a good friend of mine, and our family. Wait, is your dad a fireman also?' 'Yeah," he said. 'God, he is just up the street from my brother's place, his son Nick is right over there,' he said, pointing at me. This was Barbara's brother. The one who wants to be a lawyer."

" 'You guys are the Rossi's from New York, right?' he said. 'No way, really? Look here, Uncle Timmy is here now with his family and my family. We are sharing a place just down the boardwalk. We all come here at this time every year. I can't believe this; I just left him 20 minutes ago, and he was making coffee and cooking bacon. What a crazy world. I got to call him and left him know you are here and tell him you guys saved my ass.' "

"The ambulance guy said, 'Not right now buddy, we got to get you for some stitches.' "

"Uncle Sal said, 'Wow, Patrick, look, you go with these guys. I am here, when you get to see him, man, tell him and the family to stop by. We are here all the rest of the season. Hey, tell him I have a stash of Kern's cream soda that will bring him running. I know he loves Kern's cream soda.' "

"With that, Patrick was gone. After he left I told Uncle Sal about Barbara and just how funny this all was, because I really wanted to see her again. He asked me how I met her. I told him and that I liked her lot, but that I heard that her family didn't like Italians. He laughed and hugged me-my family were big, big huggers- and said, 'Nicky, see I know that God has a plan for you, and maybe she's the one.' Both

Vincent and I laughed. 'You're crazy, Sal,' I said. As I worked all that morning I kept on thinking how this all happened and when she finds out, I was hoping that Barbara would come, maybe stop by, along with her family."

"It was just after the lunch crunch; I was putting trash in the back when all of a sudden I heard Uncle Sal's big voice, 'God! Timmy, come here, let me give you a hug, Timmy. Why didn't you tell me you were coming to AC? Did you know we had this place? Son of a bitch, it's good to see you. Who's this young doll with you? Wait, wait, let me guess. Your name is Barbara, right?' "

"When I heard that I died. Uncle Sal was a crazy, crazy, funny man at times."

"I looked in the kitchen mirror, splashed water on my face, combed my hair and came out front. I saw her, smiled and waved, but just then a very large crowd came and we all had to stop talking and work; we made 25 sandwiches in about 15 minutes. I saw her standing back away from our stand though the side of my eyes. Barbara was watching me; just then my aunt Tess and Russ, her oldest son, arrived."

"I was washing my hands. Uncle Sal had talked Timmy in the back and gave him a bottle of Kern's soda. He talked to Tess as he walked over and got out a paper platter, put on some fries and two cheese steaks, and turned and handed it to me. I looked puzzled. He smiled and said, 'Nick, dummy, go sit in the back booth, get the girl something to drink and you go take a break.' "

"I smiled at her and asked, 'OK? What do you want to drink?' "

" 'Orange soda,' " she said."

"We walked back and sat at a table. She smiled and said that she was so delighted to see me and thought it was all too weird what happened and how we saved her brother from who knows what. She said that her entire family comes here every year and that she had been in this place just last year with her dad and mom, but never knew it was my family."

"All this time, my cousins Anna, Josephine, Tommy, Russ, Guy and Ada were all working up front, but stealing glances at us and talking between themselves. The girls were smiling and lip speaking at me with their hands as if to say 'Nicky has a girlfriend.'"

"Once again, Uncle Sal looked at all of them. He saw what they were doing and told them to work and not to worry about me. The he walked over, cleaning his hands with a towel, and sat next to Barbara in the booth and started talking to her."

" 'Hey, Barbara, so, what about my nephew Nicky here? He is something, huh? He's a good kid. I just talked to your Uncle Timmy and your Mom and they are going to leave now, but said it would be OK if you hung around here for a while. Only if you wanted, that is. So here, Nicky,' " he said, as he reached into his rear pocket, 'take your girl on the pier.'" (Uncle Sal got a lot of free passes to the Steel Pier from the folks that worked there when they came for food.)

"I looked at Uncle Sal. Did I just hear him again tell Barbara that she was my girl? I gave him a puzzled look, but all he did was smile and gently patted my face and say, 'Nicky, get out of here. You got the rest of the day off, before I change my mind. But I'm going to work his butt off tomorrow. Barbara, now go, you kids have fun,' and he got up and waved us to get up too and walked us out onto the boardwalk. As we were leaving I heard the chorus of all my cousins together saying, 'Bye now, lovers!' I turned, laughing, and gave them the finger."

"As we were walking to the pier, Barbara said, 'Oh, my God, Nick, I adore your family. Uncle Sal is wonderful.' "

"We spent that entire day on the pier, the diving horse, the bell, bands and entertainment. It was weird, but this was our first date, and I never recall ever having a better time with any girl. We walked down to the beach; we put our feet in the waves, sat on the sand talking and kidding each other. She got up, pushed me and I chased her and caught her and pushed her down in the sand."

"It was getting dark now, so I walked her home. I was surprised to find that the place she was staying with her family was just blocks away. I was going to ask her if I could see her again on Wednesday night, because Uncle Sal was going to work my ass off all day. I was all set to do that when suddenly, she turned, grabbed my face and kissed me. I was stunned and she simply said,'I will be at your stand about 6 on Wednesday, Nick. Good night.' Then she ran up the stairs and was gone, leaving me there wondering what just happened."

"I smiled all the way back to the stand and was greeted by my relatives saying, 'Nicky has a girlfriend.' My Uncle Sal just was all smiles. 'Come, get something to eat before you go home.' "

"I would see Barbara on Wednesday and every night after. That summer was particular busy at the stand; all the cousins, uncles, aunts and even friends were there. A few times at the end of the day, if we ran out of rolls, Uncle Sal would run down the other side of the boardwalk to borrow whatever he could from his competitor, who actually was his best friend Angelo."

"My cousins were happy for me. They all instantly liked Barbara and sensed I needed some free time with her, so my wonderful cousins,

Josephine, Toni, Joni and Angelia each volunteered to work my shift if I wanted. Now, I love and adored my cousins, but also, like them, needed the money."

"I saw Barbara only when I was off duty. Since my shifts varied every day, somehow she made herself available. Many times in the morning, it was making breakfast on the boardwalk, and then sitting on the beach or at night sitting on the porch of their rental or in the living room and a lot of time in their kitchen."

"Like my family, when our family rents a place, we always invite relatives and family friends to stop by. Barbara's family was the same, and I met so many of her Irish relatives. They treated me great and had a lot of fun teasing Barbara."

"On the last night, Barbara and her grandmother were in the kitchen, when I heard the front screen door open and I heard a loud very familiar voice. It was Uncle Sal. He came in the kitchen with Barbara's dad."

" 'So, here's where my best employee hides,' " he said, coming up behind me and rubbing his hand in my hair. 'Uncle Sal!' " I said, laughing and pushing his hand."

"Uncle Sal turned to Barbara's family and said, 'Folks, this is one good kid; you never have to worry about him with your daughter.' Then he said, 'Well, who's going to offer me a brew?' and he walked out onto the rear deck with the rest of Barbara's large family."

"That's how I became introduced to her family. They were and still are some great folks. That was a time and place, Atlantic City, that I will never forget. Somehow I knew then that she, a beautiful Irish girl, was going to be my wife someday."

Nick then stopped, he got up and started to walk around. Shaking his head, he said, "Oh, how I remember those wonderful days. Matt, I can hear the ocean, the seagulls and the crowds of the boardwalk, and the music from the rides on the pier."

Then he turned, looked at me and put up his hands and said, "God, I am making an ass out of myself!"

I then said, "No, Nick, I am enjoying memories, just say whatever you wish."

Nick smiled at me and said, "Anyway, on with the story. After that it seems we became inseparable. Barbara then graduated from high school, and enrolled in Saint Vincent Catholic Center School of Nursing in Queens. It was a two year course for an Associate Degree in Nursing, where she became a RN."

"I went on to attend Manhattan College and finally ended up as a CPA. I continued to work for the family while going to classes."

"By this time Barbara and I had been going together for five years now. We were both going to be 21 years old. I remember that summer when I had one more year to go. I asked her parents if they would allow me to take Barbara to Europe and visit and tour Rome and Venice. Barbara's Uncle Barney and her aunt Kelly were going also. They were to be our chaperones. This was because both our families maintained, respected and honored respect for women and the value of bonds of marriage. Barney and Kelly wanted us to go and Barney would share my room and Kelly would share her room with Barbara."

"I did this even though I had never even asked Barbara if she wanted to go. Barbara, although she never had never flown, was happy with the idea of flying. To make things worse, this was flying over the Atlantic Ocean. This was going to take a lot of persuading on my part. Her dad and mom agreed and really felt jealous. They trusted us as we had never given them reason to think otherwise. I respected Barbara. That's the way it was in those days, but things have changed now. Anyway we somehow got her on the plane and in the air, but to my surprise once we were in flight, she adjusted very well. We had a great time touring Rome and Venice; it seems we visited all the buildings, museums and churches. We ate at all the great restaurants; we did almost everything that a tourist would want to see. "

"Next we visited the Vatican City. This was important because, unknown to Barney, Kelly or Barbara, just before we left I made an arrangement with the travel agent. I obtained a small personal guided tour of St. Peter's Basilica in the Vatican City. It was a 90-minute walking tour, led by a knowledgeable Vatican Guide. There was to be only 20 people on this tour. The arrangement was that at some time during the tour when he got us all by the most holy and beautiful spot in the center of the altar, he was to stop and say, 'I think that someone has a question to ask someone here; if so, please come here.' " He would be standing in that place."

"It was a beautiful day and we all were taking this enjoyable walk. Barbara was holding my hand and was really enjoying the tour. I watched her, then we reached the spot at the point where I would have a request. The tour guide, smiling, then said, 'Ladies and gentlemen, I was told that there is someone with us that has a very important question here in this spot, before the altar of God, that he wants to ask someone. Would that person come here?' "

"As he was talking, I was watching Barbara's face. When he finished, she was looking, as the others were, to see who it was. I took her hand

and guided her though the crowd and to the place where our guide was standing on the marble steps. Then I turned, knelt down on my knee and took out the wedding ring that I had purchased and said, 'Barbara, I wanted to say here in this most holy place, before God and these folks, that I love you more than life, that I especially chose this holy spot to tell you that I love you and ask you if you would marry me, to be my bride.'"

"If there is one thing for sure I can tell you, it's that she, Barney and Kelly never expected this, and they had no idea. The look on Barbara's face could never be duplicated again. She was shocked and speechless."

"Of course the crowd was overjoyed and I heard gasps, cheers, clapping and whistles."

"Barbara just held both her hands to her face, cried and said, 'Yes!' "

"There was nothing but applause after that."

"She ran to me and we kissed. Ahhh—it feels so good to me right now to remember that precious moment. Then, as everyone watched, I slid on her engagement ring."

"Then, all the folks there whom we didn't know were actually hugging us both. Barney and Kelly had to wait. They had really no idea that I had this in mind. It was a great moment, Matt."

"Since this occurred at the end of the tour, Barbara had to sit down. She sat in the front pew and as each of our fellow tour members left they came and wished us good luck. Some talked to us in languages we did not understand, but with the smiles on their faces, we knew what they meant."

"Kelly must have immediately called home as soon as we all returned to the hotel, while Barbara and I stopped in the lobby for her to buy some souvenirs to take, because as soon as I left her and returned to Barney and my room, my folks and her folks were on the telephone congratulating me. I knew that they each had or would call Barbara also. Yes, that was one wonderful day."

Returning Home:

"When we returned home we were met by the entire combined clans of both Italian and Irish families at a party at my parents' restaurant. My mom and dad really went all out; God, the entire neighborhood was there."

Once again Nick got up and started to talk. The recorder was still running; it was like he was talking to himself.

"You know, you and I, old friend, grew up in a wonderful time. Not like the kids today. We were family. Yes, family, and we did things they just do not do today. Grandma's on Sunday for a family meal. We sat around the table, drank Uncle Charlie's wine. Ahhh, we all had respect…. but it's over."

"Any way, Barbara rented a small second floor apartment not far from both families. She and the women really made it look good. And cheap. That's when I learned about "curb furniture," you know what that is? Barbara's dad and her Uncle Mike liked to fix up furniture and things, so they would see something, a wood bed, a dresser, a chair, a table that someone put out for garbage---see—curb furniture. They would take them and refinish them so they looked as if they were new. They did great work, and it was more like a hobby."

"We were married at Saint Mary's Cathedral down town and had a great reception at the ball room of the Hilton Hotel. They say that it was one of the biggest and best weddings in both families."

"We then flew to Bangor, Maine, where we spent our honeymoon at a gorgeous ocean-front summer home of my rich Uncle Sam. Barbara and I were not into places like Las Vegas, the Pocono's, San Francisco and those other popular honeymoon resorts. Uncle Sam had a wonderful home with an outstanding view of the ocean. We spent our first morning as man and wife watching the sun come up over the ocean."

"We slept late, hung around in shorts and jeans. Toured the towns and a few restaurants. But most of the time we spent holding each other. You know, Matt".

He paused, sipped his wine and wiped a tear from his eyes.

"How that sounds so romantic," I said, "far away from the crowds."

"It was Matt. I think about those wonderful six days a lot lately" He said.

"My daughter, Connie, who I am down here with now, worries about me all the time. Her husband, Sammy, wants me to sell the house and move in with them and my two grandchildren, Shane and Juliette. She's a mom, wife and daughter. Sammy is a Deputy Sheriff in North Jersey for over 26 years now. Good man. I like him a lot."

"But I can't leave my home… you know. I am set in my ways. My son Rocky- oh, God you would love him- he owns one of the family's Italian restaurants in the city. He does very, very well. He now lives in Inwood, NY. Great house, his wife is Nancy and a set of twins, Mark and Tammy."

"Barbara and I had another daughter, Maryann; she was our first. She passed away. Matt, she died of a drug overdose. That hurt Barbara so much...to have a daughter die. She was a wild kid, Matt, but a beautiful child. She was so friendly. She was in Rutgers and where she met some bums."

Then he stopped and just looked into space for at least 4 or 5 minutes.

Seeing the tears stream from his eyes while he was remembering all this that was upsetting him, I said, "Look Nick, let's stop for a while."

He snapped out of it, looked at me, and said, "Oh, no, I'm OK. I want to finish."

"You sure, Nick? We can do this later. Why don't you go lay down for a while?" I said.

He looked at me, smiled, and said, "Look Matt, this is very important to me; you have no idea. Let's finish. I promise if I can't do it, I will stop. Please let's go on!"

"O.K. buddy," I answered, as I sat down again.

"Anyway, Maryann was living at home when this happened, she had a baby, a daughter Lisa, that she had out of wedlock. We never knew, nor could we find, who the father was. Maryann could not remember who might be the father; she was drugged a lot. However, Maryann was our baby, and so we took care of her. Our granddaughter was named Lisa. When the baby was four we found out that she had a speech problem, which caused her to hate school because the kids teased her. We took her to many doctors and they helped a lot; she was getting better and better."

"Maryann went to live with her best girlfriend not far from us and lived there for years. Then this friend got married. Maryann went to her best friend's wedding which was in Rochester, NY, where she died in her sleep. They ruled it an overdose. She had left our granddaughter with us when she went."

"It was so hard for Barbara to tell Lisa, learning that her mother died, hurting the child more. She was now 9 years old. After the funeral, we told her that she would be living with us, Barbara and me. We assured her that we would love and take care of her. God!!"

"My wife and I hurt so badly; we cried for weeks. It was very hard to lose your child. It makes you wonder if you were good parents. We were. That maybe we could have done something, but of course, we couldn't. So Barbara and I accepted it and went on with our lives."

"After that my wife and my granddaughter became so close, inseparable and more than you could imagine. They were inseparable. My wife worked with her every day, not stopping on her speech lessons. Slowly, with the help of some great speech therapists, Lisa soon was speaking like any young woman. She somehow managed to overcome it, and her speech improved so that you would never know that she ever had a problem at all."

"She became more popular at school, and our house once again became filled with the sounds of children, then teenagers. Barbara was right there with them. She helped plan parties and we had cookouts almost every week in the summer. Our house was the place these kids loved to come to. Barbara was known to all as 'Grandma'. Yes, she was in her second childhood, as I told her. Lisa grew into a beautiful young woman. She was kind, and very affectionate to Barbara, me and the family."

"Lisa was so good educationally, making the dean's list many times, that she was awarded a full scholarship to Penn State University. We were so proud of her. She wanted to major in journalism. She hoped to be a serious TV reporter. She loved the women on CNN, Fox and CBS. She watched to study them on camera actions and studied their presentations."

"We remembered her mother was so free in college that we worried a lot, but Lisa assured us that she would be safe. She was to live off campus with one of her best friends, April Long. April's mother, Rose, was a local politician and had some part of Lisa's desire. Her husband Danny was a chief investigator for the New Jersey State Police. This was a good family and they promised to keep an eye on the girls. Barbara and I were overjoyed that April was finally accepted; we were not sure until the last minute. They had a very nice two-bedroom apartment within walking distance to the campus."

"The months went by, and Barbara called her at least once a day 'to check in.' I thought that it might to too much with Barbara calling her all the time, but Lisa said that she understood and assured me that she welcomed it. I could see that Barbara was lonely and missed her, so it took her a while to adjust, but finally she did."

"Being a teacher, she was in demand and she loved what she did. Yes, there were days she would be upset and overtired, and said that she was going to quit, but this passed after a good night's sleep."

"The first Thanksgiving, we invited April and her parents to join our family, and they did. Since April was an only child, she loved our children. It was that holiday that I think Barbara became really good friends with Rose and Danny Long. After, it seems that they were always coming to my family's restaurant for dinner. It seems they knew that

I was now a part-owner of Rossi's Villa with my brother. I came in on Friday nights to help as the maître d' and they would come many times with friends."

"Knowing this, Barbara would come with me. Our father always offered BYOB (Bring Your Own Bottle) service. Barbara knew that both April and Danny loved one particular brand of wine, so she would buy and hide a bottle in the restaurant to give them and their guests as special treat."

"Those years went by so fast. Both girls were going to graduate, and we planned to go to Penn State together and to celebrate at our restaurant with all our families and their friends. Barbara and I had a special graduation gift that we knew Lisa wanted and needed. It was a brand new Jeep Grand Cherokee Sport FWD. The old Ford she was driving had seen its day. I arranged to have the dealership bring it on that day."

"Lisa, with the help and guidance of one of her counselors, got an interview with a TV station outside of Boston and she was excited. The months went by, and Lisa settled in. Month after month she became more and more confidant and was given more important assignments."

"Barbara soon took the train and would spend a weekend or a holiday with Lisa. I stayed away, giving them the time to be together. Lisa of course was proud of her grandmother and took her all over Boston, to the theater, fancy restaurants, all the sights. Barbara loved it and then Lisa gave her a key to her house.

"Then Lisa was given the opportunity to become a producer-reporter at a Fox station in Alexandria, Virginia, just outside of Washington, DC. It was filled with a lot of opportunities that interested Lisa. One of the employees of this station showed her a great, affordable, one bedroom apartment in a private house on Union street, facing the Potomac River. Lisa seemed to be more and more interested in the foreign service where she said that there were more opportunities for her."

"We, of course, were happy for her, and Lisa invited Barbara to go with her after she arranged for her belongings to be moved from Boston to Alexandria. She drove her car here to our house, left it and then she and her grandmother took a flight out of Newark to Ronald Reagan Washington National Airport. Lisa said that her home was about a 20 minute ride from there. She wanted to show Barbara how to come, because she worried about her driving."

"Lisa and Barbara spent that weekend moving her in, and then they returned on Monday. Lisa then took some of her personal items that were here, put them in her car, then drove back to Alexandria."

"We would not see her for months. On Thanksgiving she came home and then had to fly to Rome for an assignment. She had worked herself up and was being given a chance to be a foreign correspondent. She was very excited and looking forward to this chance."

"Barbara would spend every minute she could as Lisa gave her news about her days there in this city where I proposed to her. Lisa took time touring Rome and Venice; she visited all the buildings, museums and churches that Barbara had told her we went to. She ate at all the great restaurants also. Barbara loved hearing this. Barbara wanted to return some day to the place, to the very spot in the center of the altar in St. Peter's Basilica in the Vatican City. I promised her that we would return."

"A few months went by, then we got news that Lisa was in trouble. In August, 2011, she and dozens of journalists were held captive at gunpoint in the Rios Hotel in Tripoli. Lisa and these many reporters were confined to the building. It was very scary. 15 armed Gaddafi loyalists were guarding them until the final day, when it dwindled down to 2."

"Before being released, Lisa and the reporters found themselves clustered on the second floor of the building, wearing helmets and flak jackets, and guarded by men armed with many weapons. They'd sleep in packs to protect one another from being attacked and reported random sniper fire coming through the building's windows."

"Barbara could not sleep or eat. She sat there changing channels, trying to find the newest updates. It was about 3 in the morning in Tripoli when they were rescued and were taken to safety. Barbara was so relieved. She cried herself to sleep on the couch. I just put a blanket over her and let her be."

"Our phone rang at seven o'clock that evening and we got to talk to out granddaughter at last. She was in a navy hospital on a ship. She was alright; she was not hit, just a little shook."

Nick stopped talking, turned his head and started to cry once more. I stood up and walked over to him.

I said, "Nick. We are going to stop for the day. I see this is a little too much. Go lay down for a while, we'll finish this later."

"Yes," he said.

We walked slowly to the lobby and took the elevator to his floor. I got out and walked him to his room. He assured me that he was o.k. and said that he would see me at dinner. I then went to my room and slept for hours. When I awoke it was dark; I had overslept. It was a little after seven, so I got dressed and went to the dining room. I did not see Nick or his family, so I sat down to eat.

When the waiter came, I ordered some wine. When he returned, I asked if he had seen Nick tonight. It was then that he informed me that they had taken him to the hospital around five by ambulance. That's all he knew.

I rushed to the desk and tried to find out what had happened and to see if any of his family were still here, also what hospital he was taken to. I was told that he was very sick, but he was not taken to any local hospital. A doctor did come and wanted him to go to a local hospital, but his daughter said he refused and wanted to go home, so they arranged for an ambulance to drive him back to their home. The entire family then checked out and followed the ambulance.

"Did you see him? Was he awake?" I asked.

"I saw him on the gurney as they brought him out of the elevator. He was sick and they had tubes in him, that's all I saw," he said.

I was shocked. I asked if I could get his address. They said they could not give that information out, neither on him nor his family. I offered him money to give it to me, but this was a young, area college boy that kept on telling me that he could lose his job and that he needed it. I could see that he was not going to help so I went out in the sunroom with my wine and sat there thinking.

It was odd; I knew that we, two unknown men, would meet and think we would talk and record our lives and now I don't know if I will ever see him again. Would he die? If he lives will he call me and maybe, we could finish?

I stayed another day, still trying to get any information I could, but I could tell that that night clerk warned the other kids and they would not help me. So, I then gave them my name, address and telephone number in hopes they would call back searching for me. I gave them my permission to give it to anyone.

Days went by and I heard nothing. At night as I lay in bed, I relive our stories. It felt so good to me to have shared my life with Nick. Remembering felt so good. I had by now made up my mind that I liked his idea about recording my life, that in a few weeks I was going to do it for myself.

News From Nick

Months went by, and spring was here. It was a few days after Easter that I received a telephone call from Nick's son Rocky. I had never met him, but he seemed to know a lot about me. He told me that his father had passed away a few days ago. After the funeral the will was read and his wishes were taken care of, that he had one last very important wish and it was for Connie, her husband, Rocky and his wife Nancy, and his family to play the tapes we made and then to arrange a meeting with me and play his last special tape for all of us to hear. He requested that all his family and his friends be there also.

Rocky asked if he could do this at his house since it would be easier for all to attend and said that they would send a car for me. I agreed, of course, but I wondered what this final tape would contain.

So, that Saturday afternoon, a limousine arrived and drove me to Rocky's house in Fort Lee, NJ. I remembered that Nick said that he lived a few houses from Rocky and could see the New York City skyline from his lawn.

Rocky's house was a two story brick colonial with a three car garage. When I arrived I noticed that the driveway was full and there were cars parked in the street. This scared me a bit, not knowing any of these people and not knowing what to expect.

The driver pulled the car in front and opened the door for me. By that time a man and a woman were standing next to me. It was Rocky and his wife, his daughter Connie and her husband. Then their children came down from the porch. Rocky introduced me to all and I wondered why this much attention was given me.

They led me around the side of the house where there was a walk-in basement and a huge patio that was under a large wood deck. The rear of the property contained an inground swimming pool, cabana and a gazebo on a professionally landscaped lot.

There were folks standing on the patio with drinks in their hands and I was introduced then to them: his children, grandchildren, brothers and sisters, nieces and nephews, and friends.

It was Connie who took me by the hand, led me inside a huge family room with a stone walk-in fireplace. She sat me at the head of the table in a comfortable chair. There were other chairs, a few couches and there seemed to be many folding chairs scattered around the room; I could not tell just how many. There was also a beautiful wood built-in bar.

Rocky and Connie explained to me that all these people were the folks that their father loved and that he requested that they be asked to be here when I played this last tape. They said that they all heard the original tape that we made together, and from that, some knew a lot about me, along with what their dad told them about our meeting in the mountains.

Connie held my hand as she said just how much they all enjoyed the story of my life. Rocky thanked me for doing this, to which I answered that I was very happy to join them and honor his father's wishes. Rocky said that his father's last wish was for me to come and for all of us to hear this tape at the same time. This tape had never been played.

They asked if I was ready, and I said that I was and that I wanted to do this badly.

So, they started to get everyone settled. These were great people; they showed the respect and that special mannerism that only comes from the things taught by loving parents and relations.

Rocky started and introduced me once more, and it was Connie that asked me to explain just how this unusual thing came about. I told them openly just how we met, that I saw him in tears, that we just started to talk and that he suggested that we make this tape. I told them everything that I could remember including the tears he shed.

I then said that I really had no problem with them hearing about my life; in fact, was proud that they did. I said I had no idea why their father thought of this; however, I respected that their father had his reasons for recording this special tape for me and his reasons for wanting me to be here as they listened to it; but I told them that the main reason was for them.

They listened and smiled at me as I talked about my life. We stopped once to have a toilet break and they told me they loved what I said in the tape and how I felt about my wife and family. Then as we continued I watched as the tears flowed down all their faces as they talked about Nick. I told them that he had told me that he always wanted to tell them how he and their mother met, fell in love and married.

Rocky played the end of our original, starting at the place we left off before he departed the mountains.

It came to the part where in the tape I was saying. *"Nick. We are going to stop for the day. I see this is a little too much. Go lay down for a while, we'll finish this later." "Yes" you could hear him say, and then it ended.*

They all just sat there, not saying anything, just looking at the floor, out the window and the ceiling. I just watched. His words were alive in them.

Connie broke the silence "God, I never knew about how they met. It was a real true love story. I remember Mom started to tell me once."

Then, Rocky stood up, turned to me and asked if I wanted some more wine, to which I said yes. When he returned, he had in his hand the special tape Nick had recorded for me.

Nick's Tape Message To Me:

"Shall we play it now, Matt?" Rocky said, putting the tape into the machine.

"If you wish," I answered.

I then turned to his family relatives and friends and said, "I have no idea what is on this tape. This all is something I never dreamed of. I was a complete stranger to your dad and I am to you right now. But in those few hours I became his friend and felt real pleasure in hearing his story and respected him. It was his request that his children and family hear this also. So, like you, my children will hear this tape too, their father with a stranger. So, I gladly share it with you.

I then sat in a large comfortable chair they had for me and they started to listen to what their dad and I recorded. The sound was crystal clear. I sat there, sipping my wine and watching Rocky and Connie's faces as they listened.

Hi, Matt:

If you are listening to this tape the you know that I have passed. I sincerely hope that my family and friends are here with you. Thank you, old friend, for being here today.

First I must apologize for leaving you up there in the mountains. But I just had to leave. I was so overcome; it happened so fast. It was abrupt I know.

Matt, my friend, you have no idea just how much I enjoyed your life with your wonderful wife Rose. While talking and telling me your story, you described everything so well; I felt that I was there with you. It is very important at this point that I need to also apologize to you because I did not tell you that at the time we met in the sunroom, I knew that I had a death sentence and had only months to live.

I had just found out a few days earlier; no one else knew, just Uncle Sal. I did not even tell my own children. Just two days before, my doctor informed me that I had stage four cancer and that it had gone undetected for much too long, and it was rapidly spreading and hopeless now. This was completely my fault as you will see in this tape.

Thinking of just what to say to you while recording this tape and laying here in bed, I am thinking something my grandfather once told me.

He said that all of us, at one time or another, will meet a person that will be completely unbeknownst to each of us. Then by something they might say or do or something they might suggest or just some small little thing that you might see or notice in them, that this one little item or thing just might change your entire life or your complete outlook on life and different things. From this encounter, it might lead you to good fortune, good health, happiness or something. God only knows what.

I heard that this happens a lot, though it seems that only a few folks will go back to seek out that one person and thank them, so that person would never know that they were part of your success. Today in this tape, my last tape is that I want you and all the folks listening to my words that, Matt, it seems that you are that single one person in my life that has helped me tremendously, more than you will ever know. You helped me when I needed help the most.

I hope that I can make this clear in this tape. Matt, I thank you many times.

Now to why I want you to hear this tape.

*Matt, the day I left the mountains, as you know, I was just about to finish my story; in my story I think I stopped when our granddaughter Lisa was in trouble. She and dozens of journalists **were** held captive at gunpoint in the Rios Hotel in Tripoli. Lisa and these many reporters were confined to the building. It was very scary. 15 armed Gaddafi loyalists were guarding them until the final day, when it dwindled down to 2.*

We were so scared, the waiting was horrible, but then our phone rang at seven o'clock that evening. It was Lisa, herself…they were free and alright; we got to talk to our granddaughter Lisa at last. She was in a Navy hospital on a ship. She was alright; she was not hit, just a little shook. Barbara was so relieved. Barbara would really worry a lot about Lisa after that. Lisa would go on to become very successful and she received many honors. We all were proud. Barbara did not travel that much with her after that.

Then one day Barbara and I were invited to attend a ceremony at the local TV station where they were going to present Lisa with a very important award. At that time, I had been having some health problems and Doctor Sica wanted me to spend that night in the hospital for some tests. Since this ceremony was a last min-ute thing, Barbara was going to call and tell Lisa that she was going to be with me. But for some reason, I told her that I would be OK, that one of us should be there with our granddaughter, and besides, all she would be doing is sitting and waiting. I said that she could go with Lisa and come to the hospital afterwards.

The Call:

It was about 2:00 when I was in a wheel chair returning from taking x-rays that I saw my Uncle Sal, my son Rocky and my daughter Connie being escorted by

Doctor Sica into the room I was in. This scared me immediately. Why were they all here? There was something wrong! I sensed it right away.

"What's wrong, Uncle Sal?" I shouted.

He came right up to me and sat in the chair across from me. Connie came to one side and Rocky to the other.

I didn't like what I saw in their eyes.

"Tell me!" I shouted. "What the hell is wrong? Is it Barbara? I know something is wrong!"

"Dad," Connie said. "There has been an accident!"

I looked at her and threw my hands up and shouted, "What?"

Sal grabbed me and looked me in the eyes and said "Nick......Barbara and Lucy are gone!"

I stared at him.

I heard his words bounce around in my head.

"Barbara's gone, Barbara's gone."

"What? Gone? Gone? You mean dead? How? No! No! No!" I shouted. "Ohhhh God No!"

Connie and Rocky both hugged me and were crying

Doctor Sica cleared the room and retuned.

Then I looked at Uncle Sal and I screamed at him, "UNCLE SAL TELL ME",

"Nick, they were in an accident. They were going under an underpass. A gas truck rammed them."

"What? No! No! Lisa? Lisa?" I asked.

Sal said, "Nick, both are gone."

I could not breathe. My eyes were full of tears; sensations were going through me that I never felt before. I looked at the ceiling and then I felt Doctor Sica give me some kind of shot.

"Nick, I have to give you this to calm you down," he said.

I reached out and grabbed Doctor Sica, who was standing in front of me. I held him and cried and cried.

I was in bed when I awoke shortly after.

By that time Monsignor Ferrante was there next to my bed. Uncle Sal, Rocky and Connie were there too. Connie could not stop crying as she just sat in a chair.

Slowly they started to tell me what happened. They first told me that I could not see them. I was to find out that the tractor hit them from behind and exploded and that they were burned. The firemen tried but the fire was too hot and all their attempts failed.

My mind exploded; I cannot yet today explain today the agony I was going though. I wanted to scream, run, bang my head into the walls. My heart was beating so fast, this all just could not be true: my bride- my love, my sweetheart, the mother of our children, my life- was horribly burned. In my mind I pictured the fire. I imagined I saw Barbara and Lucy trying to escape. There was fire, fire everywhere. Then I sat up and screamed, " NOOOOOOOOOO!"

This was so horrible to me, and try as I could, I could not stand it, I shouted, cried, banged my hands on the bed, banged my head over and over again. "No! No! No!" I screamed at the top of my voice. Rocky tried to stop me as I tried to get out of bed. Then I felt a pain in my chest; my heart was beating so fast and I started to gasp for air.

Doctor Sica then saw that I needed to be sedated and he did.

It was very dark when I awoke. There was only a night light on. I could see Uncle Sal and Connie in chairs next to the bed. They both had their eyes shut. I had an oxygen mask on and tubes in my arms and I realized that I must have had a heart attack. My head hurt and was throbbing.

In the dark, I looked up at the ceiling. My head hurt so badly; tears started to run down my cheeks, as I cried there all alone, as I slowly allowed myself to face the reality of what had happened. It was so horrible to me, to think that they burned in what had to be a terrible way to die. I prayed and hoped that my God allowed that they both died first.

I could not stop imagining being burnt to death. Many different visions of what they must have felt and suffered could not leave me. This would be with me constantly for the next year. It was so, so horrible. I was consumed with the feeling of guilt, as I remembered over and over again in my mind that Barbara really wanted to stay home with me. I talked her into going. If I had not done that, Barbara would be with me now. God! It was my fault. I was the cause of my wife's death.

Suddenly I heard a noise and I opened my eyes and saw Connie standing there.

"Dad. How do you feel; you had a mild heart attack? You have been out since yesterday afternoon." she said as she took my hand.

I looked up at her and said, "Connie, I killed your mother."

"No, Dad, don't talk like that; you can't blame yourself," she said, squeezing my hand hard.

Then I told her that her mother really wanted to stay with me and that my big mouth convinced her to go.

"She would still be here, Connie, if I didn't force her to go!" I cried.

"Dad, Mom wanted to go. She wanted to be with Lisa. Please stop that. Please," she answered.

I closed my eyes and fell asleep.

The Funeral:

Since I was in the hospital, Connie and Rocky took care of all the funeral details. We had a joint funeral.

I was released the day of the wake, which was with closed caskets, and spent the night of the viewing in the first row, looking, staring at the caskets. Many, many of our friends, relatives and neighbors came and paid their respects. They tried to talk and comfort me, but I just sat there staring, not saying or acknowledging any of our visitors. Some as they saw my condition, approached my family instead. It was clear that I was sitting there still in complete shock.

At the gravesite, after the ceremony, I sat there after everyone parted and I cried silently. I glanced up at the sun that shined in my eyes and for a slight instant, in a flash, my mind went back to that first day on the boardwalk, I could see her. and the next wonderful few days that followed our first meeting. It was so real, her face as she was so fresh. Her laughter rang in my eyes. We were running down the beach near the waves, I could hear her voice, she was so young, so very beautiful.

Then it was broken by my Uncle Sal and Connie hope were shaking and talking to me. I burster into tears wanting to return. But agiant in a slight instant I was brought back to realty. The sun was this on my face, but I was sitting at my wifes gravesite.

Filled with tears I looked up at uncle Sal who was convincing me to leave. Everyone had left, so they wanted to take me to Rocky's where everyone went after for refreshments.

"Connie, take me home," I said.

"Dad, you should come to Rocky's; everyone is expecting you to show up. They feel so bad and just want to be there with you. Please, Dad," she begged.

"I know, I know, but I just can't do it, Connie, not now. Uncle Sal, please take me home. I want to be alone," I said, looking up at him.

Reluctantly they drove me to my house. They saw that I had some food.

"Nick, look, let me stay with you tonight," Uncle Sal said.

"No, Uncle Sal, thank you. But no. I will be OK," I said.

They left, I sat in my chair, I could not go into the bedroom. Somehow as I sat looking out the window, I how I made myself remember the many, many little things that made me love her so. After a while I went up to Connie's bedroom where I would sleep thereafter.

The Long Suffering:

This would be the begining of a long period of mental suffering for me. The daily visions of them being burnt repeatedly haunted me. I could not sleep; I could not eat. I called and suddenly just retired from my job. I became a recluse and stayed in the house. I refused help from the family and good friends. This went on for weeks, then months; I lost all track of time.

Most of the time I did not shave, bathe, clean up the kitchen, put out the garage, or take the newspapers off the porch. I just slept and drank coffee until it ran out, then I drank Barbara's tea. Soon it got to the point that I did not answer the phone nor the door. In a year I had managed to alienate myself from everyone that cared for me. I wanted them to leave me alone. I did not want their pity, I thought. I was incredibly rotten to everyone. I had encompassed myself in a cocoon of self-pity.

Uncle Sal, Connie, and Rocky came over many times and tried to talk to me. The house and the lawns that I kept so well all these years started to show neglect. Uncle Sal said that he wanted to get someone to at least clean up, but I refused and I cursed and said many horrible things to him. During this period, I said a lot of hurtful things to everyone it seems, even to my grandchildren as they tried too. I called them names, cursed and told them just to leave me alone. Then I cried, for I knew that I hurt them and that they were only trying to help me.

I would drive and find myself at the underpass where Barbara and Lucy died.

I would just sit for hours in my car and stare. At times I would sit on a wall just looking and then I would walk in the tunnel to see the place. In my mind even though I was not there at the time, I reconstructed the accident in my mind; I saw them burning. I heard their cries, My eyes saw many evil things, my imagination was unforgiving and I was overcome with guilt. It was a very busy road, yet I paid no attention to the traffic and I was honked at and cursed at. The police came many times, different officers, and would tell me to stay out of the road. They warned that I could be arrested, so I promised that I would, but didn't. Once I slept in my car for three nights, not eating, just drinking bottled water.

I was sleeping in my car one night. It was very dark and early in the morning when the police came. They took me to jail and towed my car. They called Uncle Sal because they knew him and wanted to waive any charges. Uncle Sal wanted to take me home, but the police instead placed me in a hospital, and had doctors examine me, over and over. I was there for three days, then they gave me pills and released me. I would return to the bridge. I was sleeping there for four days when once again I was arrested and Sal came to bail me out once more. This time he took me home.

The house was trashed and smelled very bad. Uncle Sal started to clean up. He put me in my bed and left for some cleaning supplies. He stopped at McDonalds and bought me three cups of coffee and two sausage and egg sandwiches.

He made me come and sit with him at the kitchen table. At that time, hungry, I enjoyed the sandwiches and the hot coffee. Uncle Sal had always been a good friend to Barbara and me since we met. I watched as he sat at the kitchen table, looked at me and cried, too. He held my hands,\ even though I fought him.

"Nick, please, you can't go on like this. Look, it was not your fault. Things just happen. Please eat these and have some coffee. Damn it, you know Barbara would not like this," he said. He took the lid off of another cup of coffee and

handed me a sandwich. I looked at him. Just kept looking. Not saying anything, just looking, for a long while. Then I brought my eyes up to his. I looked into them, said, "Why, Sal?" Tears burst out of my eyes and I reached out and held him. "God! I miss her so! Why, Why, Why?"

Uncle Sal just stood up and held me. He stroked my back and said, "I don't know, Nick, only God knows," and he started to cry. I never saw or heard Uncle Sal cry so much. We sat there for what seemed like hours. There was a knock on the door. Sal got up to answer it. I heard footsteps and then, "Hello, Nick." There was a very familiar voice.

It was my next door neighbor Vicky Bernstein. Vicky was a girl that I had known all my life. Vicky McCauley was her maiden name. Vicky had lived across the street from my family and her dad was a captain in the local police department. We were the best of friends and Vicki was one of the only person in my life that always seemed to have a positive effect on me. She always found a way to get to me. Her father and mother were like my adopted parents.

She married Bobby Bernstein, another boyhood friend who was a commercial pilot for United Airlines.

For some reason, today, I welcomed her visit. Vicky was a person that I never could control. She always knew how to get to me.

"Look at you, Nicky, better yet, smell you! Look at this place! Sal, take him in the bathroom and see he shaves and takes a bath. I got some cleaning to do."

With that, she walks over to me, puts both hands on my face, looks me in the eye and says,

"Nicky, Barbara would not like what you are doing. You are hurting yourself, your family. For God's sake, we love you. Please don't fight me; I've known you too

long. I'm here and I am going to help you if you like it or not." With tears in her eyes, she continued, "Don't fight. Now go take a bath."

That is how I started to return to being myself. Sal and Vicky stayed and cleaned and fed me.

Uncle Sal stayed all night that first night and made me breakfast the next day. After my bath, my shave and putting on some clean clothes, I was glad that he was there. He was very sensitive to my feelings and stayed away from pushing me or discussing things that might hurt me or set me off.

It was Uncle Sal and Vicky just talking to me those few days that made me realize that, ever since the funeral, I had pushed away, insulted and pissed off all the folks that I loved so much. I really did not realize that I did. In my personal grief, I managed to do things that I never intended to do. I was ashamed.

Vicky came over for four days, bringing food and homemade soup. She cleaned and when Uncle was not there she would sit and just talk to me. I thanked her over and over again.

"Nick, you now have to behave yourself. Bobby and I are flying to Charleston for a few days. You going to listen to Uncle Sal? Promise you wouldn't go nuts again? Please, I don't want to come back and kick your ass," she said, holding both her hands to the sides of my face and looking straight into my eyes.

"I promise, Vicky; go enjoy yourself," I said.

She gave me a smack on the top of my head, kissed me and then, shouted, "Remember, Nick, you promised!"

After she left, I looked around and saw that my home was clean once more. I walked out and sat on the back porch with a beer and I slowly I started to recalled the many, many terrible things I did and said. I was so ashamed. I felt so bad. I needed to rectify anything I could, somehow.

Somehow in my act of self-pity I had forgotten that my son Rocky and my daughter Connie had lost them too, and that my grandchildren had lost their grandmother. Plus, all her family and our friends and neighbors all had the same grief that I felt. God, how could I have been so selfish. God! God! How could I have not realized what I was doing? How could I now ever apologize or make this right again?

As the days went by, I slowly became more visible to folks. But I slowly discovered that I was a coward, for each time I saw someone that I knew that I should apologize too, and I started to, somehow I couldn't get up the courage.

Getting Sick:

One day, I had a very bad cold and I could not stand up. I managed to get to the couch and because I really felt so bad, reluctantly I called my son Rocky, who came over. It was on a Sunday and he called Doctor Sica who, after asking Rocky questions, told him to take me to the hospital. But I could not stand, so Rocky called the doctor, who called an ambulance.

They took me to the emergency room where I thought that they would give me some drugs for my back and my cold and send me home. In the hospital they took x-rays, took blood and took many tests. Rocky stayed with me until my daughter Connie came. Finally, Doctor Sica came and told us that I had a bad cold and that he was going to keep me for a few days to take tests. So they admitted me.

In the next few days, they took blood samples all day and in the night also, more x-rays and many different tests for the heart and so on. On Tuesday evening Doctor Sica stopped by. He told me that after another x-ray in the morning, the was sending me home. He then said that he wanted to see me on Friday, to call and make an appointment. I was so happy; I felt better and I had no love for hospitals.

I called his nurse for an appointment. She said that the only time he wanted to see me was Friday at 5 o'clock, which was his last appointment of the day.

So I drove to his office and apologized to his nurse for anything I might ever said or did while I was crazy that might have offended her.

She took me to his office, not to the usual examining room as in the past. I thought that this was very unusual. I sat in the leather chair and waited for the doctor. He walked in with a large orange envelope in his hands.

"Hi, Nick," he said, sitting behind his desk.

"Hi, Doctor," I said.

Then he looked at me in a strange way I did not recognize.

"Nick," he said, "because of all you were going through with losing Barbara and Lucy, and your heart problems, I didn't want to add to your problems in the hospital, plus I wanted to be very sure before I talked to you today."

Then there was a knock on the door and the nurse came in and said, "Doctor, his Uncle Sal is here." I was shocked. Why was Uncle Sal here? I thought to myself.

"Send him in," he said.

Uncle Sal then walked in and sat in the chair beside me. Something was wrong I knew, bringing me into his office instead of an examining room and having Uncle Sal here.

"Doc, what the hell is going on here?" I said, standing up.

"Nick, please sit down," he said.

"Look, Nick, as I just said before, because of all you were going through with losing Barbara and Lucy, I didn't want to add to your problems in the hospital, plus I wanted to be very sure of everything before I talked to you today. And, I wanted your uncle to be here. It was true that you had a very nasty cold. But as we tested you, we discovered something else. Something that you must had have for a

while and never knew it. But as I said, I did not reveal this to you because of your condition and because I wanted to be positive of our findings."

I was shocked and I looked at him. What could it be?

"God damn it, tell me, Doc," I said.

With that he took some x-ray film out of the envelope and turned on the light and placed the film on it.

He turned to me and said, "Nick, I won't kid with you. It is bad, very bad. Our tests have discovered that you have cancer. It is in your body, it is what we called stage four cancer, and it is very bad. Yours is a very rapidly growing kind, and already has infiltrated your liver."

"Cancer?" I asked. "Are you sure?"

"Nick, you are one of my oldest friends. Yes, I had five of my best fellow physicians confirm my findings. It is positive. No, Nick, there is no mistake......God, Nick, I wish that I didn't have to tell you this, but I kept it too long from you now. Nick, as I said, this appears to be a fast spreading kind and I am afraid there is no treatment for it. Nick, you don't have much time.

Uncle Sal grabbed my hand. I turned to look at him and saw his face. This was the face of a tongue twisted man that I knew loved me but was lost for any words that he could say to comfort me. He just did not know what to do or to say to me.

"Nick, knowing that I had to tell you this, wishing it was not true, I asked your uncle to be here for you. I hope you don't mind. I am so sorry, my friend....... Look, I am going to leave you both here....... take your time......Please.... Ohhhhhh," With that, he left us alone.

97

I was completely numb; how could this be? Was this all just a bad dream, but now I looked at Uncle Sal next to me. It was real.... We sat there for a few moments in complete silence.

I heard Sal breathing hard, I saw tears rolling down his cheeks. His eyes squinted and I saw the hurt in them. He was squeezing my hand. He looked at me with that helpless look.

I pulled my head in my hands.... bending over...all this was penetrating my mind; I was dizzy, it was hard for me to breathe. God, why? I was going to die. Why, me? Why did God take my Barbara, my Lucy and now me? What had I done to deserve this? We always were a good church-going family. Why has God allowed this? Is there a God? Is there a God?

I felt as if I had no legs, no strength, no sight.

Stunned, suddenly I stood up, and somehow walked through the empty waiting room, with Uncle Sal behind me saying somethings I did not hear. It was all a blur. Doctor Sica took my hand, but I shook him off and just kept on walking into the sunlight. Just walking, not looking at where I was going and not caring. I did not hear anything, even though this was the busiest street in the community.

Somehow, I walked over to a bus stop bench and sat down. My mind was racing, then parts of our past went through my mind. My life was there before my eyes. I saw Barbara, my children and grandchildren, smiling, laughing, Christmas, Easter and vacations. I held my head and laid on the bench. Then without warning I felt a surge of hate developing.

God had failed me. I was being punished for some unknown reason. At that point, to me there was no longer a God. I turned my back on him and the church.

Home:

The next thing I remember was that I was in my living room lying on the couch with Uncle Sal sitting next to me.

He was talking and slowly the blur faded and I heard.

"Nick, talk to me, go on, buddy say something. You are scaring me," he said.

Suddenly I focused on him and for some reason I sat up fast, grabbed him with my two hands and said, "Uncle Sal...I don't want anyone to know, no one. Please promise me, tell no one. Can you promise me that, Uncle Sal? I never asked you for anything, promise me!" I said with tears in my eyes.

"Sure, Nick, but.....but what about your kids, your grandchildren... they should know...God Nick......Doc Sica told me as we were leaving you only have a few months...shouldn't you tell them?" Uncle Sal said, standing in front of me.

I looked up and said, "Uncle Sal...no one. Please...I will handle this...tell no one"

"OK, OK Nick," and he kneeled in front of me and kissed my forehead. "God, I wish I could do something, anything."

"I know, Uncle Sal, I know," I said.

Uncle Sal then called his family and told them that he would be spending Saturday and Sunday with me. He lied and said that he was helping me do some work in the house.

I went to my room and sat in my chair, just sitting there with my eyes closed.

Uncle Sal came in with some coffee and a bottle of water.

"Are you alright, Nick?" he said. I just kept my eyes closed and shock my head.

"Look, I was going to leave you alone here, but I'm staying. I am not leaving you; I will be out here if you want me, Nick. Just call. Anything you want, just call. OK?" Again I shook my head and he was gone. He would from time to time come check on me, but I would still be in my chair.

That night I sat there for hours looking out the window in the darkness at the street lights and the headlights of cars on the road. I could not sleep. My heart was filled with such pain, my mind could not stop asking why, why, why. Barbara and I tried and were always good people. Why did God do this to me?

Slowly in those hours before the sun rose on Saturday my heart was slowly and uncontrollably filling with hate and I slowly no longer believed that there was a God.

I walked into the kitchen. Uncle Sal I saw sleeping on the couch. He must have been very uncomfortable; he was a large man. He was in a deep sleep. I made some coffee and sat on the back porch. Soon I heard him stir and soon Uncle Sal joined me.

He poured a cup of coffee and sat. I knew that his eyes were on me, but I did not look up. I told him that he should go home now.

Looking only into my cup, I thanked him for caring and taking care of me. I told him that I have spent the night accepting my fate and that I was going to be O.K. Once more I made him promise not to tell anyone, that I wanted to handle it.

Uncle Sal spent the next few minutes telling me that he wanted to stay, that someone should be with me at this time, and he insisted that he was staying. Slowly I reached over, put my hand on his and slowly lifted my eyes to his and said.

"Please, Uncle Sal."

He looked into my eyes, stopped what he was about to say, put his other hand on mine and said, "OK, Nick, if that's what you want."

With that, he gathered his belongings and went out the back door. I heard his car pull away.

My Plan:

From that minute I started to design a plan. My mind started to twist in looking for some evil scheme. It seems now that all the strength and self-confidence I ever had, died. I no longer wanted to live. I knew all the last days of pain and suffering that this cancer may bring me, I was just not willing to try to endure it. Then my mind slipped back and once again, as I did many times in the past, I imagined the pain and suffering from that fire that Barbara and Lucy must have felt. It was so real, and it hurt to think that they should have died in such a horrible way.

I was so twisted that I was not thinking of my family for some reason, my self-pity had taken control of my mind. Then I remembered a pistol that Uncle Sal once gave me that he used to keep in the restaurant. It was downstairs in an old safe under my work bench. I remembered it had no bullets for safety for the kids, so I had hidden the bullets up in the attic…and I knew they were still there.

Yes, I will get it and kill myself. Even though I knew suicide was against God's laws, tears were streaming down my face. I was crazed, full of hate for everyone and uncaring for the unknown things would happen to me so fast in the next few days.

Then, exhausted, I managed to go to my room and after almost three days I finally fell asleep.

My dreams were full of hate. I saw images of my daughter Maryann, Lucy, my granddaughter's mom. Barbara and Lucy. In my crazed desire to hate, somehow I had totally forgotten my daughter Connie and her husband Sammy, and my grandchildren Shane and Juliette, Rocky, his wife Mancy, and the twins, my grandchildren Mark and Tammy.

Then, as I said, unknown to me at that time, things would happen so fast in the next few days.

Starting My Evil Plan:

The following morning, Connie and my granddaughter Juliette came in the back door. I was still in bed.

I was really so afraid that Uncle Sal might have broken his word and told Connie. I sat up on the side of my bed. Connie came into my room, kissed me and started to tell me that they had stopped and brought me some milk, coffee, bread and things.

From their faces it did not appear that they knew. Juliette started to put the food away, and Connie was going through the house picking up things and complaining that I should be ashamed of myself. I was assured that Uncle Sal had not talked to them. They both then went on cleaning up.

Then Connie announced that she had to go pick up Shane from baseball practice.

It was Juliette that came to say goodbye and said, "Grandpop, we are all going to the mountains for a weekend, with our next door neighbor and their kids. Would you like to come? Oh, say that you will, please!"

"Juliette, your grandfather doesn't want to go with us," said Connie.

Without thinking, I said, "I might, Connie."

"Oh, great grandpop!" screamed Juliette, and she put her arms around me.

My daughter was shocked. She quickly walked out of the kitchen, looking at me and sat next to me. "Really Dad, would you go?…you need to get away; it will do you good," she said.

"Do you have room for me?" I asked.

"We would make room, Dad, wonderful!" Connie said. "We will be leaving Friday morning, staying until Monday night, four days, Dad. Want me to come help you pack? You'll love this place."

"No, I can pack myself," I answered.

Then they left.

My thoughts were that when we got there, I would take a walk in the woods and shoot myself. At this time, as you can tell, I had lost all sense of reality. Looking back at it now, it seems that I gave no thought or consideration to, if I had done that, what it would have done to my daughter and my grandchildren, my family, friends and neighbors. It seems that none of that mattered; I was so consumed with hate and being willing to die. My mind was no longer my own.

Matt, that is where I meet you.

If you remember in the lodge that night, when you walked into that room in the dark, I was sitting there crying. Unknown to you was that I had the pistol in my hands under my sweater on my lap and I had just finally convinced myself to get up, walk over to that sunroom door walk into the woods and shot myself. I wanted all the minutes, hours and days of the horrifying visions and the screams I have heard in my head constantly since they died to stop. I had come to the end of bearing it. I had to stop it. I was minutes away, from my evil plan, when you walked in.

Yes, my friend.

But then you started to talk. I heard your voice Something stopped me and I listened to you. The voice of a complete unknown stranger to me. But for some reason I still do not understand, I asked you, "How long has it been?" I asked how long ago your wife died.

I remember there was silence. We both were looking out at the lake.

Then you said, "Rose, my wife and I, after the kids married and left home would love to come here to see the autumn leaves. She would collect a lot of leaves and she put them in books. They are still here; you know…. just can't get myself to throw them out. She loved to collect four leaf clovers in the summer. So this morning, I thought I'd get away for a few days and relax."

At that second, I took the pistol out of my sweater and slid it back in my pocket and the insane idea I had to leave faded. I have no idea why.

Then I think that I told you that I was here with my daughter, her husband and my two granddaughters and their friends for four days. We just arrived today.

Then there was silence once more.

Then you continued and I said, "My wife loved the food here, especially for some reason their breakfasts. We would get up early, walk all over the lake, come back and sit on the restaurant's patio outside tables and enjoy the early sun. My wife loved their blueberry pancakes."

What you said penetrated my mind, because Barbara loved to do the same thing. Not knowing because it was so dark, you did not see the tears in my eyes. I pushed back in my chair and relaxed and somehow my mind cleared. I remember my words: I told you that Barbara and I also loved the breakfasts after our walk, sounds like we did the same things. And I told you, "By the way, my name is Nick Rossi."

You talked about the way we remember all those little things that didn't mean much before, but now we love to remember. Then you said that it was very hard for you today, and that you had a such great memories and all day long, you had been remembering many years ago. I remember your words were, "I have been remembering many years ago when I first met her in a playground, we were just kids then. I don't know why, but early this morning as I was sleeping, it all came back to me. God, I could see her, Nick."

I was not really sure just why I was sitting there, once hell bound to kill myself. Talking to you a man, a total stranger, about this. But it felt so good talking to someone.

But like I said, for some reason, maybe God sent you, but you.... for that particular moment, I both needed and wanted to talk to you. I remembered that we drank and talked about our wives and our families. I could tell that you were a man like myself that truly loved his wife as only a man could, and in many ways we were the same. We parted and made a date for breakfast the next morning.

As I went to my room, it seems that something, I still do not know, but something you did or said started to change my thinking. As I lay in my bed, I realized what I might have done tonight and it was then that it dawned on me just how horrible my shooting myself would have been for those grandchildren and my daughter. How could I have ever gotten myself to even consider it? I could not sleep, thinking that it might be best to just tell my daughter, Sammy and the kids this in the morning.

As I lay there also I was so interested in hearing your life story because some-how deep inside me there was something telling me to find out more about you. I had brought with me to record a last message to my children a tape that I brought yesterday. It was then that I had the idea, that if you would agree, we could both tell out life stories, raw, uninterrupted. Of course, you did.

To me your story was so great, I felt the love that you had, I heard the love that you were given, in all the words that I heard you speak into the tape. Your words were so descriptive that I really felt that I was there with you. You had a wonder-ful, amazing life, my friend. I have never enjoyed a conversation more than ours.

That last night when I was telling you about Lucy, suddenly I could not help crying.

You, my friend, suggested that we stop for the day. You asked me to go lay down for a while. Caring about me, you walked me to my room. I remember I told you that I O.K. and said that I would see you at dinner.

It seems to me that right after that while I was talking to my son in law Sammy on the phone, I must have passed out. They called the doctor and of course I had to confess to him and my daughter that I had cancer. He called Doctor Sica who arranged for a local ambulance to bring me back home. My daughter and grandchildren were hurting as it was hard hearing about that this way. They allowed my granddaughter to ride in the back with me.

Of course I was drugged for the two hour drive back home to the hospital. But I remember waking and feeling more relieved than I had felt in over a year. I felt an inner peace that I had prayed for. I had completely understood things that I should have never let fester as it did.

In my bed once looking up at the ceiling of that hospital, I asked myself just how I survived those horrible months. Once more, my friend, my grandfather's words returned; that all of us, at one time or another, will meet a person that will be completely unbeknown to each of us. Then, by something they might say or do, or something they might suggest, or just some small little thing that you might see or notice in them, that this one little item or thing just might change your entire life or your complete outlook on life and different things.

While recording this to you today, Matt, I cannot point out any or the one thing you said or did, but you are that one person my grandfather talked about. Meeting like we did, at that moment that may have caused me to commit that sinful act, the way you talk, the things you said, your life's story; whatever, there was the something. That something.

As a result of our conversation and understanding that God has his ways, remembering all the wonderful things God gave both Barbara and me, I knew that I lived a great life with the woman meant for me. I tried but failed to list the many, many blessings in life, my wonderful children, my precious grandchildren, my family and friends.

As a result, you have indeed changed my life and gave me that different outlook. I first went back to God. Then one by one, with a happy heart, I reached out to each and every one that I offended and made peace with them. The feeling I have is indescribable.

So, Matt, my friend, although we had known each other only three days, I want to thank you and I want you to know that I am now with Barbara, Maryanne, and Lucy.

God bless.

Now, Matt, finally, since I hope that my family is here and listening to the tape I requested you share with them all, and since these will be the last words you might ever hear of my voice, I would like to end this tape, as unusual as it might be, with the following,

To my lovely daughter Connie, my son-in-law Sammy, my son Rocky and his lovely wife Nancy. And to my wonderful affectionate grandchildren Shane, Juliette, Mark and Tammy. I know that over the past weeks, we have talked and said our goodbyes.

However, over the years, your mother and grandmother was always the one for saying the right words and spoke for us both.

But she is not here, so I need and so much want you all to know and to remember that there is, nor never has been living, a father and grandfather in the history of the world that has loved and been so proud of you all than I.

Each one of you over the many years has made our lives complete.

I know now that all that has happened is part of God's plan. In my heart I know I will soon be with my Barbara once more. There are many things in my story that I know you had never heard.

Yes, these tapes you heard are very unusual I know.

However, it was so very important to me that you all hear about your mother's and my life. I knew that I could never have the time to remember everything and it was always hard for me to tell you each face to face what I felt you should know. With Matt's help, I have relived those wonderful years and in my mind I have given you all at one time forever our true love story. I hope that you will always remember just how much we loved each other.

Goodbye, and God love you.

The tape then ended.

As it ended, there were tears all over the room, but no noise. It was Rocky that said, "Matt, can we have a copy of this tape?"

"Sure, Rocky, I will make a copy for all that might want one," I said.

As I sat there, looking at the family he loved so much, and his family and friends around the room, my mind raced back to the day Nick first proposed this idea to me in the mountains. At the time I thought it was bizarre, weird and crazy. But somehow it intrigued me so much that I did it with him. All he really wanted was for his family to hear all about his and Barbara's life in the hope that they would enjoy and share it with others.

As I looked around the room, I could see that his plan was really working; call it a crazy idea if you want, but I don't think anyone this room will ever forget these tapes.

I was honored by the many thanks I received from his family, friends and neighbors and especially all of his grandchildren, but I thought that it was time for me to leave and to just be together remembering what they had just heard. I left. Uncle Sal and Rocky hugged me and said that from now on they wanted me to be a part of their family.

I will always remember the faces and the cries of this loving family as long as I live. Of course Nick. He was a good proud man and he did what he wanted to have all of his family and friends to hear. As the lights on the New Jersey Turnpike rolled by while I was being driven home, I thought hard to myself about just what occurred tonight and just how it happened. How in those few days in the mountains, two troubled men from different paths and different lives met, at the same time both came bearing heavy thoughts of their departed wives, pain that they only could feel about the women they both loved and adored so much for so long. Each having a special and interesting true real life heartfelt love story to tell. Yet, both felt no one in their families was interested in hearing the wonderful heartfelt stories they so desperately wanted to share with their families..

That one of these men was within just minutes of committing suicide but somehow was diverted by this simple meeting.

That all of what happened since that day was simply because two strangers could have met there in those mountains and began a simple casual conversation that unfolded into what happened tonight.

I then began to wonder just how I could present our tapes to my family. Somehow I think God might have been behind this.

The End

Made in the USA
Middletown, DE
18 October 2023